COLD SUMMER

MY BROTHER'S KEEPER

THE FINALE

A Novel by
Courtney B.

To submit a manuscript for our review,

email us at

submissions@majorkeypublishing.com

Chapter 1

Where We left Off

"Chance! Chance!" I could hear Choyce yell, but he sounded far away. When I tried to focus, it was like I saw him at the other end of a long dark hallway, and he motioned me to come back his way. I was a little responsive but slowly faded in and out of consciousness. I could feel two or three people lift me up and put in a car.

As I walked down that same dark hallway, I could hear bro's voice.

"Don't go to sleep, lil' bruh, stay with me!" I kept closing my eyes, I just felt like I had to make it down that hallway, but Choyce's voice made me stop every time I heard it.

"Stay with me! Don't go to sleep," he kept repeating.

I knew when we pulled up at the hospital and parked because I heard him get out and call for help. As soon as they put me on the stretcher, I completely faded

4

out. I couldn't hear my brother's voice anymore. I was surround by the brightest white light that I had ever seen.

I could hear mumbles that sounded like prayers but, I wasn't too sure. That was when a conversation started about me. I could hear clearly but couldn't participate in it.

"So, what do you think about him after all this?" I heard.

"He's going to make it." The conversation went on.

"What? What do you mean, he's already right here?" It sounded as if it turned into an argument.

"I know, but, it's just not his time." It was the final say.

After I heard those words, I came back to consciousness. And as soon as I opened my eyes, my body shook uncontrollably.

"Nurses, hold him down. He's going into shock!" I could hear the doctors say as I was being held down. I didn't know what they did, but my body was stuck and couldn't move at all.

*****

Three days later...

"It's okay, baby, you can wake up now. Mama's right here," mom said as she leaned over my bed to kiss my cheek.

"Where am I?" I questioned. I yelled in pain as I went to move my arm.

"Just relax, you're in the hospital, babe. You've been shot," she explained as she pressed the button and asked the nurse to bring me more pain meds.

"You got grazed on the side of your head, but your shoulder and arm were a direct hit. The doctor said you're going to be just fine," she said as she helped me sit up.

"Wow, everything happened so quick. I'm just happy to be alive," I said as a nurse came in and gave my something for my pain, then held a straw up to my lips.

"You are blessed, baby, and I'm am very happy you are too. There were some detectives that came up here and left their card. They want for you to give them a call when you woke up," mom explained.

"Well, I'm glad I was sleep through all of that. I'm still amazed the doctors said the bullet just grazed my head. Because I could've sworn, I got hit point blank. At least that's what it felt like, but I thank God," I said because I felt that, he'd spared me that time.

The pain medicine had started to kick in, so mom helped me lay back the way I was. When I closed my eyes, I felt mom kiss me again then leave out the room. An hour had passed, and I woke back up.

"Hey, Mr. Coleman, glad that you're awake," the doctor said as he walked into the room.

"What's going on Doc?" I questioned as he hung up the x-rays of my gunshots.

"We'll, I wanted to go over the damages that those bullets caused," he said as he sat down in a chair by my bed.

"Well, I hope they aren't too bad because I have to head off to school in a little over a month. I'm attending Alabama University to play football," I said with confidence.

"Your mom told me all about it, but I don't

think you'll be able to play this season until we perform surgery," the doctor said.

I couldn't believe my ears; my entire world stopped. That pain hurt worse than my gunshot wounds.

"Excuse me, I thought I heard you say, I'm not going to be able to play football this year." I just knew I heard him wrong.

"I did say it, but once we restructure your scapula, you should be able to get back out there. It's just going to take some time to heal," the doctor said as he pointed at the x-ray of my shoulder.

"Your mom told me that you're a running back. I can't see you taking too many hits in college and last until you get to the league without surgery," he explained.

I was speechless; I had no words. I saw nothing but red and wanted my revenge. Those nigga's drove away with more than just my car; my dreams were in there with it.

"I'll give you time to think, but a couple of detectives wanted me to call them when you were alert. So, I'll do that then come back for your decision." As the doctor left the room, I laid my head back, and tears ran down the side of my face.

"Get up, lil' bruh, it's time to leave. We got your clothes, so come on," Choyce said as he and Muhammed rushed to get me dressed.

"Watch his arm, Muhammed," Choyce said after they helped me put my shirt on.

"I got it, just put his shoes on his feet." They had gotten me completely dressed, then placed me in a wheelchair and rolled me out to the car.

"You good, Chance, are you focused?" Muhammed asked.

"Yeah, I'm straight," I replied.

"Alright I'mma need for you to stand and get into the car." I trusted bro had a reason for getting me out of there, but it was just too much going on. My head started to pound instantly. I stood to my feet and got into the back seat of the car.

"We found out who did the shit, lil' bruh," Choyce said as he put his car in drive.

"Yeah, it was some hoe ass niggas from my

hood over on 42nd," Muhammed said as he looked in the back seat to see if I was focused or not.

"Yeah, well those niggas fucked me up from playing football next season. Now, I want to fuck up they souls. And if they are from your hood, then why the fuck were they after me?" I questioned with aggression as I tightened up my head bandage.

"They thought they hit a lick. Back in the day when I first opened up, I used to have people steal cars and bring them to the shop. I paid top dollar, so I was known for that kind of come-up."

"I hadn't done it in years ever since, I met my car plug from Houston. The niggas that car jacked you, bought the car straight to my shop."

"They thought since I was big homie, that I'd pull a play for them, off the strengthen we were from the same hood. I saw the car pull up from my office camera. So, I pressed the button to let you in. The front end was all wrecked up, so I thought you had gotten into a finder bender," Muhammed explained.

"One them got out, the driver's seat with your

chain in their hand. I saw that had blood on it, and I was terrified. I didn't know what happened."

"They were like, 'O.G., we just car jacked this nigga.' Bragged about how they killed you, wanted me to fix it, and change the VIN number," he went on to say.

"I played it off, like coo. Let me go calculate the damages to see how much I'll charge you. I only got a pump in my shop. So, I grabbed it. Once I came out, I fired at them, and I missed by inches. They ran like some bitches, that's when I called Choyce," he finished.

I knew bro wouldn't have let him make it this far if he were lying, so I believed him.

"He was there, when they called apologizing and shit," Muhammed said.

"It's was too late for that shit though, them niggas shot my little brother. Now, I'm just finding out they almost ruined his dreams! I want they blood in puddles behind this!" Choyce demanded as entered onto the highway.

"Didn't we just buy a house over there on 42nd?" I questioned as looked out the window.

"You took the words right out my mouth, lil'
bruh," Choyce said as he looked in his sideview mirror to
switch lanes.

"Ironically, the house that we got on 42nd is
directly across the street from where those niggas be at,"
he went on to say.

"I want you to see how I ride for mine, so all
while you're healing up, Muhammed and I about to post
up at the house just to see how they move."

"Nah, for real. I can't wait for that one. I damn
near want to go right now," I said as I looked down at my
arm, then thought about the surgery that the doctor
suggested.

"Nah, you heal up, bro. We got it all worked out.
When you recover, then we will go in," Choyce assured
as he exited the highway.

"Real talk though, Channy, she ah fuck keeper,
bro. She came up to the hospital every day until she had
put ah fuck nigga in his place. She was like, 'Look, my
dude just got shot, get the fuck out my face.' When he
still tried you talk to her. Yo, she went off so bad, she got

12

banned from the hospital. Unique and I were on facetime weak as fuck. He better be lucky I wasn't there." Choyce laughed as he pulled into our backyard.

Mom considered us grown, so she moved out, and her and Troy got a condo downtown. Ever since she got with him, her life elevated in every area. I'd even noticed how strong she was in the hospital when she had come to see me. I really appreciated Troy for that.

Mom let us have the house; it was still hers, and she showed up when she wanted just to make sure we kept it clean. She raised us right, so we kept it spotless.

*****

A hit for the Hitman--Saturday July 4th

I had just woken up and walked into Choyce's room to see what he was on.

"Hold up, lil' bruh, I gotta line this play up," he said as he made a call.

"Hello," someone answered with a deep sinister tone.

"What's good, this is Choyce, Muhammed's guy. He told me we got the same problem. I got ten bands for you right now," Choyce said.

"I already talked to cuz. I'll meet y'all at the spot around 5:30," the guy agreed.

"Say less, then," Choyce said.

"Bet, say no more."

"Who was that, bro?" I questioned.

"That was Muhammed's cousin, Hitman, he did six years in the joint. Those same niggas fucked him over before he got locked up," Choyce explained.

"Muhammed said he was on some murder for hire type shit, so I hired'em."

"Fuck it, then less blood on our hands, it's ah play," I said as I left the room to take my shower.

I'd waited on that day for two weeks. Choyce and Muhammed had been watching them niggas' every move the whole time. All while I was in the shower, I visualized their demise, and I wouldn't miss it for the world.

As soon as I got out, Channy called my line.

"What's up, babe, how are you?" I couldn't help it. Even with everything I was going through, her voice put the biggest smile on my face.

"I'm fine. Just wondering how my babe is feeling today."

"I'm feeling much better. I went to my check-up the other day, and the doctor said that I'm healing up better than expected. I still need surgery, but I was glad to hear that," I said as I rebandaged my arm and shoulder.

"Good, I'm glad too, but my family is having a barbeque, today. It's my going away party, and I wanted to come pick you up, so we could chill out."

"That's coo, come through. I'm ready whenever you are," I agreed as I managed to get dressed without any help.

"I'm on my way, okay?"

*****

Knock at the door

"What's up, babe? I see you don't be playing behind that wheel," I said as I walked out of the house.

I turned to lock the door and turned back around into a soft kiss on my lips.

"I missed you, babe, and I'm really glad that

you are feeling better," She said as she adjusted my sling, and we walked to and got in the G-Wagon.

As we pulled up, it didn't look like that many people were there.

"Come on, I got something that I want you to see," she said as walked in her house and up to her room.

"I've been thinking about us a lot here, lately," Channy said and brushed her soft boobs across my back as she shut her bedroom door locked it.

"What's been on your mind, I questioned?" As I turned to look at her, she had this look in her eyes that I never seen before, out of all the years I'd known her.

"I want for you to be my first and my last. And today is the day I want you to take my virginity," she said and started to take off her clothes.

She got completely naked and stood in front of me. She had the body of a Goddess.

"Babe, if this is how you want our first time to be like, I'm all for it. Just know this is my first time too. I can't think of any other woman, I'd rather do this with. I got you, babe, come here."

She helped me out my shirt, and I kicked off my shoes. Then, she pulled down my shorts.

"Please don't hurt me. This thing is huge," she said as she bent down and put her lips on the tip of it. I could feel her soft tongue circling around it.

"Damn, don't stop. That shit feels good," I said as I closed my eyes and leaned my head back.

"You like that, zaddy? Let me spit on it for you," she said when I looked down at her. She looked up at me, spit on it, then jacked me off.

"I love this shit, babe, keep going," I said as she put the head back in her mouth. Her head bobbed in a sexy motion as I looked at the top of it.

"Let me please you," I said as she stood up then sat of the edge of her bed.

I got down on one knee as she put her hands behind her legs and held them for me. I put my nose close, and her pussy smelled like water. It was the same color pink as her lips, with a fat clit.

I used my tongue to rotate around her clit. When I slipped it in her hole, I didn't get the same reaction. So, I went back up and focused on her clit some more.

"Oh, zaddy. Yes, baby, stay right there, please," she moaned aloud.

I looked up and saw her eyes were shut tight as she pulled on her nipples. I kept working her clit with my tongue. Her pussy had gotten super wet.

"Oh, my God, yes. Babe, keep doing that, I think I'm about to explode. Fuck," she said.

I closed my lips on her clit, then flicked at it with the tip of my tongue.

"Oh, oh. Oh!" she screamed.

Her stomach moved in and out as if she were breathing heavy. She pushed my head back then pissed all in my face.

"What the fuck?" I questioned as I stood to my feet. I grabbed the nearest towel.

"I'm sorry, babe, but it's natural. I've never done it that way before. It was so much," she said as she got out the bed to help me wipe off.

"What's so natural about pissing in my face?"

I questioned and felt disrespected.

"No, babe, I squirted on you," she said as she walked me back to the bed.

"Like I said, it's natural."

The way she got back in the bed had my dick was hard as a rock. That freaky shit had me mad for a second. The thought of how sexually her body moved before it happened, had me wanting to make her squirt again.

"Are you okay? Come here," she said then laid on her back.

"Yeah, I'm straight, babe. I'm back focused now, open your legs," I said as I carefully climbed in her bed. I had to watch my arm.

"Are you ready?" I questioned as I put the tip of it right at her hole and began to work my way in.

"Oh, shit. This is fucking crazy," she said as she opened her legs wider and closed her eyes tight.

It was super tight, but the more I stroked in and out, the wetter she got. My head finally went in first, then the neck of it followed.

"Ooh! My! God!" she screamed and made all kinds of uncomfortable facial expressions.

"Be quiet," I shushed, but she wasn't trying to hear none of that.

"I can't! It's too big, oh shit, hurry up. Please, babe, please!" she screamed louder.

I tried to pull out, but she wrapped her legs around me, so I couldn't. It went all the way in, and her walls hugged my dick so comfortably. It felt so warm, soft, and wet, that I could feel myself about to release.

"Let me up, I think I'm about to cum," I said with my eyes closed. She still wouldn't let go. I looked at her, and she was trying her best to look back at me. I could see the pain and pleasure in her eyes.

"Let me up, Channy, it's coming out," I said.

"No, give it to me, zaddy. Give me all of it," she demanded and slightly moved her hips.

I couldn't hold it any longer, I released in her so much, my body shook and scared the fuck out of me. We had sex for the first time, and I'd came inside of her.

I scooted to the edge of the bed and tried to stand, but my inner thigh muscles were throbbing. I just climbed back in and laid next to her.

"Where did you learn how to suck me up like that?" I questioned with a serious look on my face.

"Porn," she answered with her devilish half-grin.

"Where did you learn how to work my clit, nigga?"

"The same for me too." We couldn't help but to laugh.

After we finished getting dressed, we went back downstairs.

"I hope we weren't too loud," Channy whispered then winked as we noticed her family starting to show up. Once again, her sense of humor had me weak as fuck. The way she walked towards the kitchen didn't help either.

After we ate a plate of food, Channy and I went back upstairs for round two. I had to hit it from the back that time, and after we finished, I laid in her bed. She had her head on my chest and it dawned on me.

"Oh shit, can you drop me off right quick?" I asked. As I sat up, a quick pain shot through my arm because I moved too quick.

"What's wrong, do you need to go back to the hospital?" she asked because of the way, I held my arm.

"Nah, I just gotta meet up with Choyce at 5:30," I answered and got out the bed. She helped me get dressed then got ready herself.

"Come on, babe, let's go," she said as she grabbed her key and purse.

She dropped me off, and when I walked in the house on 42nd, all I saw was a six-four, 450-pound big black dude that stood in the front room with Choyce.

"Perfect timing, lil bruh, this is the hitman, he's about to make it happen for us," Choyce announced as he walked over to shake up with me.

"Off top, good looking out. I'm Chance, by the way," I said as I extended my hand to shake up with him. Muhammed had just come from out of the back room with a money counter.

"Count up, lil' cuz. These are my guys; they like to

pay they weigh." He grabbed the ten bands from off the table in the living room and started his count.

The last beep from the money counter indicated all the money was that there. Hitman then sat down in a chair in front of the window. He just looked at the closed blinds. Choyce had just come back from out the kitchen and stopped in his tracks.

"What the fuck is he looking at?" he questioned then looked over at Muhammed.

"I don't know. I told you, he be on that some Michael Myers shit," Muhammed answered.

*****

He'd been sitting in the same spot for going on an hour and a half. We'd been stopped paying attention to him.

"What's good, my nigga? What, you don't know how to open the blinds or something?" Choyce finally broke the silence as he stood up and yanked the cord to open them up.

"I'm mean, shit, it's going on two hours since you counted up. Make good," Choyce demanded.

Hitman grabbed his bag and pulled out a jar full of clear liquid, then sat it on the table next to him. He then reached into his pocket and grabbed his pack of Al Capone cigarettes and took three out.

"Man, I know this nigga ain't about to get high first," Choyce said then covered his nose with his shirt.

"I told you, lil' cuz was from the 32nd block over on the west side. All niggas on that side of town is crazy as fuck and smoke wet sticks all day, every day," Muhammed explained as Hitman twisted the lid off the jar, and the smell of embalming fluid filled the room.

Muhammed, Choyce, and I stood back with our noses covered to see what he was about to do next. As if we were watching a scary movie, he dipped all three of his of his cigarettes in the embalming fluid then smoked them back to back.

"This nigga is crazy, for real," I said as he started to move in slow motion.

Hitman looked out the window and saw the targets pull in the driveway, then went to the side door. He unzipped a big ass bag then pulled out a Mossberg double barrel sawed-off pump and a Draco.

"Time for me to go to work. It's show time," he said slowly as he cocked the pump and walked out the house with his guns exposed.

"This nigga can't be serious?" Choyce questioned as we looked out the window.

He walked across the street and kicked then door open with one stomp. All we heard was the Draco going off.

"Yo, the fuck is going on?" one of the niggas yelled as he ran out. He jumped to make it down the three steps to the side door, but the Mossberg pump caught him in the back in mid-air, and he flew into the house next door.

Hitman walked the last one out the house, then had faced him towards us and made him get down on his knees. We saw him plead for his life. Hitman squeezed the rest of the Draco clip into him.

"Damn, he cold for that shit!" Choyce said.

Muhammed grabbed the AK from out of the closet.

"What's that for?" I questioned.

"Shiid, just in case he come back over, trippin off them wet sticks.

"That nigga cold than ah mufuckah. That last one must've been personal," Choyce said again and was stuck looking at the way Hitman stood over the last dude's body.

"What's wrong wit'em, Muhammed? How'd he get so fucked up?" I questioned.

"He ah product of a broken home. His parents ran the neighborhood, we grew up in. Until one day, this jealousy ass nigga hired a hitman to kill both his parents, so he could take over. They got murdered when he was six years old. By the time he was twelve, he killed the hitman and the one who ordered the hit," Muhammed explained as he closed the blinds and ran out the back door to ride out.

*****

It was 3:30 in the morning, and I laid in my bed in the pitch black. I was in so much pain, I couldn't go to sleep. I turned my phone off all day after we pulled off that hit on them niggas that car jacked me. I just needed time to myself. I thought about football, surgery, Choyce, and his crazy lifestyle. I also thought about Channy. I couldn't believe I came in her twice.

I wasn't ready to be a father yet. I hadn't even gotten the chance to live out my dreams yet. Right when I was about to close my eyes, she facetimed me.

"Hello, babe, what's good? You okay?" I questioned. She was on the other end, crying so much that she couldn't even get a word out.

"Babe, why are you crying? What's wrong?" I sat up as I hoped, I didn't hear any bad news.

"I just saw the news, babe, and it was saying some guys got killed by where I dropped you off at. Your phone was off, so I couldn't locate you or nothing," she said as she looked off to the side like she'd replayed something in her mind.

"I just got scared because I haven't heard from you since I last seen you. I felt the same way I did the day you got shot," she sobbed.

"I'm sorry for not calling you, babe. I could've at

least let you know that I was okay. I'm just going through a lot right now. I just feel like I'm losing my dreams for nightmares," I tried to explain.

"I hear you, but you don't understand. I feel like the night you got shot was my fault. I almost lost my man because of me, and now, every time that I see the news, I'm an emotional wreck." Channy was emotionally tied to me. At that time, I didn't realize how deeply in love she was with me. I had to let her know she wasn't to blame for that night.

"It wasn't your fault. I was just in the wrong place at the wrong time, so don't let that trouble you. And as you can see, we're facetimein right now. So, that should let you know that it wasn't my time, and if anything, you saved my life that night."

"How, Chance? How did I save your life?" she questioned.

I could see her emotions calm down because of that statement, and I honestly believed what I had said.

"Your love, babe, your love surrounded me so strong that night, it stopped the bullet that could've ended me," I assured her.

"Chance, promise me that you will never leave me. Promise me that you will always love me and grow old with me."

My mom showed me unconditional love and that could never be replaced. But outside of her, I had never had someone else that cared so much about me like Channy did. And I had never felt the love that I had in my heart for anybody but her. Those were only feelings that soulmates could share with one another.

"I promise you, Channy, that I will never leave you. That I will always love you, and that I want to grow old with you," I said as I looked her in the eyes. I could see her worries go out the window.

"Babe, I meant every word that just came out my mouth, and I'll back up them all up."

"Chance, you know that we had sex twice, and you came in me both times, right?"

"I know, babe. It just felt so good, and I couldn't control myself."

"What if I'm pregnant?"

"Then that means, I will have to accept my responsibilities and become a father to my child. Also, a husband to the woman that will give birth to it."

"Babe, I'm so glad that you're still alive. I went through so much when I thought my last memory of you would've been the last time that I kissed you," she said as her tears had started to roll down her face again.

"Babe, so far, I've been kidnapped, and we bounced back from that. You got shot, and we bounced back from that. Then, I got shot, and we're still here. Our love is too strong for this earth to separate us. So, you stop worrying before you get gray hairs all over your head," I joked just to see a smile on her face.

"Okay, zaddy. Will I be seeing you tomorrow?"

"I'll do you one even better. How about us seeing each other later today?"

"You know what I meant. I'll see you later, bye."

"Okay, beautiful." I truly had loved Channy, and I could tell that she strongly felt the same way about me. I had a virtuous queen to sit beside me on my throne. I felt like it was time to take us to another level.

Chapter 2

Choyce wanted to meet with me at our club to brainstorm on our next power move. Any other time, I was all for coming up with a plan to expand our entrepreneurship, but not that day. I had received some bad news.

"What's wrong, lil' bruh? Usually you're on point with the ideas. We've been here for thirty minutes, and you haven't said a word," Choyce stressed his concern.

"I'm just fucked up right now. I went to my checkup to discuss my surgery. The doctor told me I might not be able to play football again," I answered and was heartbroken.

"The fact that I wasn't shot in a shootout or from running in someone's house for revenge, but it happened while I was minding my own business, troubles me. They just didn't know; I would've let them have the car. They didn't have to try to kill me for it," I said as my emotions got the best of me.

"Lil' bruh, nothing in life is promised. You have a dream but who's to say, one day you could've got hurt on the field. Or suffered a brain injury that you couldn't bounce back from. Everything happens for a reason. Don't beat yourself up about it though," Choyce said.

"Look, ever since Justin turned me onto this lifestyle, I knew it would be away for us to make it regardless. I remember the first time he counted ten bands out in front of me. We were in middle school. He told me, he never spent money because he was trying to see one hundred bands."

"My goal is to see a billion and that's why I save to this very day, in memory of him. I took to this field like you did to football. I didn't want to ride the wave of your dream. But I wanted to be there for you, until you made it to where you wanted to be in life," Choyce explained.

"Lil' bruh, look at it this way, we're young black businessowners. Not to mention, we have high school diplomas. All I know is, I've been investing the money you made from the couple licks you pulled with me. It's been collecting interest as you would say."

"It was half yours anyway and by us not taking what we have for granted. We have made a lot of money and haven't done a single count up on it," Choyce said.

As I held a pen over a blank piece of paper, I got an epiphany.

"Thank you, bro, I needed to hear that. While you were talking, my wheels were turning. The question I have for you is, how are we going to make our next move, if we don't even know what we are working with?" I asked and Choyce just sat there in a blank stare.

"I did my math, and we have three stash spots, seven trap houses, and a club. Let's make our rounds just to see exactly how much we have. We can bring it back here count it, then we can go from there." Choyce and I shook up then started our rounds.

*****

Three days later

"Fuck this shit, bro. We're about to hire an

accountant!" Choyce said as he threw a stack of money on the floor after the money counter went crazy and started spitting out money everywhere.

I'd lost count after seven-hundred and fifty thousand. I had no idea Choyce was out there getting it like that. Every time I counted a hundred grand, I looked at him like, "Who the fuck are you?"

"Nah, for real. That's exactly how I'm feeling right now. I thought it was a good play, but this is way too much money," I replied as I kicked my feet up on the desk.

"This still ain't it though," Choyce said as he looked at the money counter like he wanted to shoot it.

I looked over at him like, "Are you serious?" As I looked around our office, I saw that the safe was filled with money that we hadn't even counted. The seven mail carrier boxes filled with money we hadn't counted, plus the seven-hundred and fifty bands we had stacked on our office desk.

"Bro, how much more do you have? I mean, this looks like more than enough money to make our next move. Can't we just leave it there?" I inquired. I felt like if we bought any more money into our office, it wouldn't be enough room for us.

"Nope, we still haven't checked on any of our trap spots. Niggas owe, and it's time to collect," Choyce insisted.

"You got to be fucking kidding me. I'm telling you, bro. Let one of them niggas act funny like they don't want to pay. The way I'm feeling right now, I might have to pop one of'em," I stated as I stood up, ready to go.

At that point, I was ready to take my frustrations out on anyone that got out of line with me or Choyce.

*****

It was twelve p.m., and Choyce had made rounds to six of the trap spots. Choyce showed me how he checked niggas and put the fear of God in their hearts.

The more aggressive he approached each power move, he made; the more respected he was. He told me that's how he brainwashed niggas into soldiers.

It was going on four days, and we needed some rest. After I took a shower, I was out like a light.

"Ride with me, lil' bruh, we're about to go check-up on them niggas we saw at the club," Choyce said as he opened my bedroom door.

"Say less," I said as I look at the time. It was five o'clock in the morning.

When I made it to backyard, Choyce had just put two AR-15 guns in his trunk. That was an indication them niggas was on some bullshit.

"What's good, bro? They're not trying to pay up or something?" I questioned.

"Hell, nah, I've been calling these niggas all morning, and they keep sending my shit straight to voicemail. I called one of my slimes. He told me that the bricks that we got from Black are selling fast, and they're over there making a lot of money. They already on their third brick and only paid twice," Choyce explained.

"Say less, bro," I replied.

We pulled in the ally and parked two houses down. The neighborhood was quiet, and it was still dark outside. We looked at the house, and all the lights were on.

"Come on, bro. I'm trying get in and out," Choyce said as he passed me ski mask and we got out. Once we got the AR's from out the trunk, we proceeded towards the house.

It was one of our rental properties, so I had the key and used it to unlock the back door.

"I don't got nothing to do with it. Y'all can play with them if you want to, but the way I was raised, never bite the hand that feeds you," we heard someone say as we crept through the kitchen. Is was a fat dude on his phone with his back towards us. Choyce wasted no time.

"Hang up, nigga, toss your phone on the table, and put your hands in the air," he said with aggression.

"Damn, Quan. I really thought you was solid, but you folded on me. Start talking before I kill you," Choyce demand and gave Quan chance to come clean.

"Man, Choyce, I told them dumb niggahs not to try that shit with you. They blocked your numbers and shit," dude hurried to explain in his defense.

"They let niggas from the hood influence them to turn on you. They just took one-hundred bands to go buy from my nigga a few hours ago. The rest of y'all shit is in the basement," he said as he pointed towards the basement door.

"Lil' bruh, stay up here and watch the door," Choyce said as he shoved Quan in the back towards the basement with the muzzle of the AR.

"Hurry up and take me to my shit!" Choyce demanded as Quan walked towards the basement door.

His hand shook as reached for the doorknob. He was hesitant to turn it, and Choyce fired a round into the ceiling.

"Bitch! The fuck you acting so nervous for! You trying to set me up or something?" he questioned as he took a step back and took aim.

"Nah man, I just don't wanna to go down there if I'm not make it back up. I did right on my end by you. All I'm asking is that you don't kill me," Quan pleaded.

"Show me where my shits at, and I'll let you live, nigga! That's the best I got for you," Choyce negotiated. They went into the basement.

"Where's it at, fuck nigga!" I heard Choyce

question.

Quan was talking too low for me to hear what he was saying in response.

"What, nigga? Is this it! What, you think this shit sweet! Hurry up and pack this money."

Quan's phone lit up with a notification. When I swiped on it, the message read, "Aye, bring the rest of that to this address, fuck that nigga. We got a new plug."

Right before I could let Choyce know that nigga was trying to play us, I heard five shots come from the basement.

"Come on bro, let's go," Choyce said as he ran up from the basement. I grabbed Quan's phone, and we ran out the house.

*****

Choyce set the navigation to the address, and when we drove past the front, all the lights were out. So, we circled the block and came up through the alley. We saw the lights in the back of the house were out too, so we pulled into the backyard.

The sun had started to peak, so we had to make

a quick move.

"Come on, bro, let's check these windows and doors right quick," Choyce said as we got, out then worked our way around the house.

"Everything is locked, bro. How the fuck are we going to get in?" I questioned. We walked around the entire house and ended back where we started.

"I don't know, but our mufuckin money in there," Choyce said as he stomped the back door, and it didn't even move.

Choyce was ready to give up. I just so happened to look up and seen a piece of a curtain flap out a window when a breeze blew past.

Look up, bro," I said and pointed at the window. It was about fifteen feet up.

"That's too high to jump up there. Man, shit!" Choyce yelled.

I looked around to find something to stand on. I spotted a ladder laid long ways on the garage next door.

"We in, bro. help me out right quick, you know my arm fucked up." I said as I ran over towards it.

"I didn't even see this bitch," Choyce said as he grabbed ahold to it, then we walked it over to the house.

We climbed in through a bedroom and immediately saw weed, coke, and heroin.

"Oh, shit! Start tossing this shit out the window, lil' bruh. I'm about to locate the money," Choyce ordered and ran out the room.

"Bet," I agreed, but instead, I took the cover off the bed, put as much as I could in it, and dropped it all together. I did the same with the pillowcases and sheets.

I left the room and entered the master bed, and he had more shit in there. I got as much as I could and tossed it out the window too.

I climbed back down, pulled the car up, and popped the trunk.

"Lil' bruh! Come here and help me," Choyce said as he opened the back door. He stood there with five large duffle bags.

We hurried to throw them in the back seat. We then filled the trunk, reversed out the ally, then sped away.

We drove to Choyce's stash spot and put everything up. Then, we headed home. We knew it was a matter of time before the police found out about Quan. He was dead in the basement of one of our properties.

"Stay here, bro. I'm going back over there to play it off like I had to check on some repairs, then call the police," Choyce said as he got ready to take a shower.

"That's coo, bro, just move smooth. Let me know how it went," I said then went in my room, so I could take mine next.

Choyce had been gone for an hour. I had a little time to myself, so I could think, but I lost all hope. I wanted to play football but that wasn't going to happen. My dreams had been shattered.

"Snap out of it, man," I said to myself as I saw myself in a full-fledged pity party.

No matter what I tried, I couldn't take my mind off it. I grew angrier, the more I thought. I wanted to hurt people like they'd hurt me. I wanted to take from people in hopes it ruined their dreams like someone had ruined mine.

I feel heartless without a care in the world. I decided as I got in the shower.

*****

Choyce came back about three hours later and knocked on my door.

"Bro, the police were already there by the time I pulled up!" Choyce panicked.

"Damn, what they say?" I questioned as I stood to my feet. His reaction had me nervous.

"They basically said that there was a murder at our house, and the police charged it as a robbery gone bad. They found a lot of evidence deeming it drug related," he answered and sat on my bed.

"No shit," I laughed.

"So, we just robbed our damn selves," I said as I thought back on the shit.

"I can't lie, lil' bruh. It was risky in doing so, but that's what I need for you to do from now on. We goin on anybody, that's trying to play wit us. We just gotta move smooth," Choyce explained.

"Ain't nothing wrong with collecting what belongs to us, and if the count isn't right, then we taking what doesn't. Off top!" I said as we shook up.

*****

Choyce and I pulled up to the gas station in our hood and posted up, so we could talk. We wanted bounce plays off one another and enjoy the weather. It was a beautiful day, and we just felt like being out. Somebody pulled up on us out the blue.

"Man, I heard that you two are out here pushing weight," dude said as he got out and approached us.

He was dressed casual, nice drip game, and had a street nigga vibe. He didn't look like he was on some bullshit.

"We holding. What, is you tryna shop or something?" Choyce questioned.

"I'm Delyn, and yeah, I'm tryna shop. So, what's good?" he said calmly.

"What type of move were you tryna make? I mean, you want somethin big, small, soft or hard?" Choyce questioned as he looked dude eye to eye.

44

"I want the soft, but I need a kilo though," Delyn said but seemed a little nervous.

"Is that it? You better get what you can now because I'm almost out," Choyce suggested to finesse the sell.

"Shit, bro, I got to know the prices first. What they goin for?" He questioned.

"Seventy-five bands all day long."

"Damn, bro, that price is too high, but if it's as good as people say it is, then fuck it. I'll take two," he agreed.

"Alright, bet. When you need them by?" Choyce asked as if dude was goin to say later in the week or something.

"Right now, if you got them on you," he offered like he had the money up front.

"Nah, we don't keep shit on us. But take my number and drop your location," Choyce offered.

"Alright bet, I'm sending it now," Delyn said as he locked bro's number in, then got in his car.

*****

We went to the stash spot and got a couple kilos from the lick we it earlier that morning. I grabbed a Desert Eagle, and bro had his Draco. He also pulled out his pump and an AK. It was something about that moment when dude got nervous. That made us take extra precautions, but we still went because scared money don't make no money.

"Lil' bruh, you drive your shit. I'm going to ride with you," Choyce said and gave me a look like he had second thoughts.

We followed the GPS, and it took us to an apartment complex about thirty minutes away.

"Lil' bruh, keep your eyes open just in case we gotta go to work, you hear me?" Choyce mentioned to make sure I knew what to expect.

"I got you, bro. Let's just get this shit over with," I said as I parked my car in reverse a few spaces down from the apartment building.

"Off top, we are, but however this shit goes, we just gotta make sure we're ready for whatever," Choyce said as he reached down, cocked his Draco, then put it in a backpack.

"The pump and K are in the trunk with the kilos, just in case," Choyce said as they popped the trunk to get the keys.

"Lil' bruh, put one in the chamber right now. Stay a few feet back though, and when you get to that tree stop walking. That's your cover if we get into a shootout. That's if though, I got a feeling, and we should be coo," Choyce instructed as we got out the car then walked around to the trunk.

Choyce already had his Draco in his backpack. So, he put the keys under his shirt and cuffed them with his hand.

"I got you, bro," I said as I cocked my gun, then placed it on my side under my shirt.

We walked towards the apartment, and once I was near the tree, I did exactly what Choyce told me to do. That's when Delyn came out the building.

"Don't freeze up on me, lil' burh. If it goes down, it's either us or them," Choyce explained.

"Why he staying back? Is he nervous or

something?" Delyn said and laughed.

"Nah, why you as that?" Choyce questioned as we checked our surroundings.

We then knew it was some bullshit involved, when a couple other apartment building doors opened.

"Yeah, bitch! Y'all killed Quan! You niggas breaking in house and shit! It's a wrap for you niggas!" one of the lil niggahs from the club yelled out as he busted out a building. He held an AK-47 with the long clip and cocked it back.

"You niggas are too fuckin greedy! I got two keys right here, you can have these bitches!" Choyce yelled out and threw them in the air to avert every one's attention. They watched the powder fall from the sky like it was snowing in the middle of July.

I had no time to waste. I quickly pulled out my gun and blasted at dude that held the AK in his hand.

"Keep shooting, bro!" Choyce yelled out. He had his hand on his Draco, but it got stuck in his backpack, so he started shooting through it.

I ran behind the tree and covered him as he shot

his way back towards the car. It was just too many of them coming out the apartments. All I could see was doors opening as niggas ran out shooting.

As bullets riddled the tree I stood behind, I fired as many shots as I could, in hopes Choyce made it to the truck to grab his AK. I only had five rounds left. All I was doing was making people take cover because my aim was off, and I hadn't shot anyone. I just needed to avert their attention off Choyce while he handled himself with the Draco.

"Come on, bro!" I heard Choyce yell as he fired a gang of shots towards the opps. I knew he'd made it to his AK. It forced some to get back into the building and others to take cover.

I was about to take off running but a bullet blew a chunk off the corner of the tree right by my face.

"Bro! Come, on!" he yelled out again, but I panicked because I was getting shot at.

I just took off running from behind tree, like I was about to score a winning touchdown or something. I got near the car closest to me and took a leap of faith.

"You good, lil' bruh?" Choyce questioned as we were both pinned behind some cars. He quickly reloaded the K with an extendo.

"Yeah, I'm good," I said as he cocked it and slid the K over to me. He picked up his all-black twenty-gauge shotgun.

"I got you covered, lil bruh, get over here and start the car up!" he ordered as I noticed the shots stopped for a second. They had to have been reloading. I stood up and took aim in the direction I last saw the opps at and pulled the trigger just in time.

"What now, fuck nigga!" I yelled as they were headed towards us like we ran out of bullets or something. As I made my way towards my car, Choyce stood up and let Delyn have it with the twenty gauge. The damage he did was frightening.

"Come on, bro, let's go!" I yelled as I put the car in drive. Choyce ran over and hopped in. I looked for the opps, and they were all gathered around Delyn with their hands on their heads in disbelief.

I peeled off then hit the highway.

*****

It was two weeks later; Choyce and I had been moving drugs in heavy rotation. He had people pulling up from in town and out of town like clockwork. I saw why Choyce never counted his money, it just came in so quick. Who had time to keep up?

He told me,

"That's how you know when you out here getting to the money, lil' bruh. When you make so much of it that you can't keep count."

We were on another level with selling; we changed our numbers every two days and moved from house to house. We took all the house out our names, like we sold them and put them other people's names. We invested in our own lawn care service, roofing company, and construction company. We were able to hire a contractor, and he already had his construction crew. So, we launched our own websites, to hire our staff to fill the other positions.

"Lil' bruh, we leave for Jamaica in seven days. So, we need to make a move to secure our money and drugs while we're gone. I can't have ah nigga running off in our club or stash spots. Just because they don't see us going in and out. The Library is full; I couldn't put nothing else in the if I wanted to. Besides that, I can't think of another good hiding spot," Choyce stressed his concern.

Choyce had our construction company remodel The Library. It looked just like a functioning Library, but every bookshelf was filled with the kilos he got from Black. I considered how much money was coming in and our lack of storage space. I was able to come up with an idea.

"You must've read my mind, bro. We need something like our own warehouse. I got just the place to find one at, too. The Housing and Community Development public hearing on South Meridian Street. It's about to open in a couple hours. Let's go," I suggested.

"Bro, I can't lie, you're the brains behind all this shit. I thought about everything under the sun but what you just said. Set the GPS, we're on that right now,"

Choyce said as we got in his car and drove off. We bought seven houses: three on the east side, two on the west side, and two more out south.

We called our contractor and invested in the remodeling and selling part of the house. The warehouse out north was our new trap spot. It was six thousand square feet, with plenty corner space for a cheap price.

"I just called Muhammed, lil' bruh. He got a U-Haul, so we'll be able to start moving our shit asap," Choyce explained as we took a tour through our new investment.

"Off top. I just dread the fact we're about to haul, all the shit back and forth. That's a lot of money, drugs, and guns, bro," I commented.

"It all comes with it, lil' bruh, relocation is the most important part," he explained.

"I feel you, let's get to it." It took us five days considering we had to move late night into the early a.m., but we managed to secure all of it in our warehouse. We then were ready to fly to Jamaica.

Chapter 3

Norman Manley International Airport,
Kingston, Jamaica

"Wah gwan?" Black questioned.

"We just landed at the airport," Choyce said as we stood in baggage claim, waiting to receive our luggage.

"I'm already here," Black answered Choyce then slid a note to one of airport security officers. He then escorted us to past the customs process and out the airport.

As we walked out, we were greeted by a convoy of black tented-up Suburban SUVs. Three in front of a black stretched Suburban and three in the back of it. I already felt welcomed.

"We made it, Black, now show us what goes on in Jamrock," Choyce said as we got in the stretched Suburban and shook up.

"No doubt. I'm glad to see that you made it," Black said as he lit up a blunt, hit it twice then passed it to Choyce.

"Did yuh give dat letter to customs?" Black questioned, to let us see how much pull he had in his country.

"Yeah, when they saw it was from you, they let us right through." Choyce laughed then took another pull from the blunt and passed it to me.

"Gud mi told yuh dat everting would be fine," Black explained with a smile that showed off all thirty-two of his platinum and diamond teeth.

"Off top, so where are we going from here?" I questioned. For the first time in a while, I felt free from all the hatred back in my city. That vibe felt soulful.

"First, mi gonna show yuh the more peaceful part of Jumdung," Black mentioned as he pointed out the window.

"Right now, we are riding through Trench Town, home of de legendary Bob Marley," he explained.

I looked out the window at the streets of Trench

Town. I saw dirt roads, metal shacks, and condemned buildings, and those were people's homes. There was trash debris and broken bricks waist-high on every corner.

It was clothes that hung on clothes lines and people everywhere. That was when I noticed, it didn't seem to bother them any. No matter their condition of living, that was their community; they loved, and cherished what they had.

"Bob Marley was a Rasta man dat believed in peace," Black said as he pointed at a life-sized mural on a brick wall that had been painted in his memory.

"The politicians did nah like him fah dat," Black went into further detail.

"He wanted to liberate the people through his music. He taught us that we need to stop fighting our brother and love each other. One love, one heart for everybody."

"That made it hard for the politicians because they were in power, and the more divided they kept the people, the longer they could run a corrupt system, and they had him murdered because of it," Black shared a brief history with us about the legend.

The more we continued to roll through Trench Town, I saw that although they hadn't received the life luxuries like we had in the US, they were their own source of government within their community. They found their own happiness outside of their corrupt government.

"Now, mi guh fi tek yuh dung town," Black explained that he was about to take us through the downtown area.

Downtown had Choyce and I stuck as we looked out the window. In America, we found pride in what we had. It wasn't the same in Jamaica. They found pride in just being alive. Everyone lived off the resources that they had access to and didn't carry the weight of a struggle on their face. I could tell that they made the best out of what they had.

"Down here, the murder rate is ten times higher than it is in the USA," Black said as he'd finished rolling another blunt.

"What makes people just kill like that? That sounds like some senseless shit," Choyce questioned as we looked out the window, at a part of the world, we had no idea existed.

"Understand this about Jamaica, twenty percent of us live below the poverty line."

"Only de fittest of de fit survive. As long as you stay fit, then you will survive," Black answered.

"Are you from around this part of town?" I asked.

"Mi cum fram Bennet Lands, my garrison. In de very heart of Kingston, Jamdung," Black said as we come to a complete stop. We were then in his garrison.

"Come on, I'm about to walk you through my turf."

As we got out of the car, we had at least fifteen other people with us. I looked around, and it's like I was in another world, and I loved it. I could feel the spiritual strength of ten lions. I felt as if my aura was surrounded by the soul of survival and wisdom.

That trip was a blessing to me. Choyce and I followed Black inside of a duplex style home. Black walked us through the process of how he got the kilos shipped out, then took us to a back room.

"You are in a serious place, right now. Daily, you wake up and see people dead in the streets. We have to protect ourselves before we go any further," Black explained as we entered a back room. It had kilos of cocaine, pounds of weed, wooden crates filled with guns, grenades, and missiles everywhere.

"Likle broad roll up de high-grade ganja," Black told his little brother to roll another blunt.

He went over and got a few ganja buds from out one of the pounds then started to roll up spiffs.

"You said that you and your brother have much respect back in the US, right?" Black questioned Choyce as we all sat at a table.

"Yeah, we earned our right to do what we do on the streets. It was a lot that came with it though," Choyce answered with confidence.

"Here, respect only goes so far, doesn't matter who you are. Here, it's live by the gun or die by one," Black explained as he walked over to one of the crates, that had the guns in it.

"Take this, you and your brother," he said then handed us a couple.

"Damn, Black, what kind of Uzis are these?" Choyce questioned as he received his with open arms.

"Dis ah Israel Uzi. Yuh like dat one, du yuh?" Black questioned if we liked them.

"Off top, these mufuckahs go hard than a bitch," I said as I held it in my hands and looked over.

"Like is an understatement. I love this bitch," Choyce said and cocked a bullet in the chamber.

"Good, because with this, you will be more than respected," Black said as he passed the blunt to Choyce.

"Wen yuh shoot dis gun it's lacka lion roaring in de jungle. When people hear it, you must make them back up, and respect who you are with no title."

"There's one more thing that, you need to know about these guns. And that is here, we're our own government."

"And we must protect our garrison, that's the only reason we carry them. Do you understand what I am saying?"

"Nah, for real. I feel what you're saying though. Hit this shit, lil' bruh," Choyce said as he passed the blunt to me.

Black didn't know that we did that shit for a living. Having a gun just made us feel more at home. After we smoked a few more blunts, we hit the streets.

"Now, wi a redid to waak inna fi mi yardie," Black explained that we were about to walk through his community. We left out of the backway and followed the roads.

Black walked us through his garrison and told us how he became a Mega Don in Kingston. Besides the fifteen people that came out with us, each step we took, the more people came out of nowhere.

They greeted Black and welcomed us. We we're just a few miles up the road, and it looked like a we were a part of a parade with music and all. The women danced so freaky, it had Choyce and my full attention. That shit was so sexy.

That was the first time I'd ever smoked, and that

ganja had me high as fuck. I looked so focused and aggressive, and that attracted the woman to me even more. But like I said, when we first arrived, I strongly felt the spiritual presences of that country and it embraced me.

"Don't fret mi won't be here long, mi affine patrol fi mi garrison," Black explained for us not to worry, he just had to patrol his area.

"Since the Babylon mon won't do it, he just wants the money. De politician won't do it him just won't de votes. Me and my gang will, I provide all sorts of resources for my garrison."

Black explained that the policeman was money hungry, the politicians just wanted votes to remain in office, and no one cared about the people. Him and his pittas had to be the ones to supply all necessities to his garrison.

"Nah just fi fambily de entire community." He said not just for his family but for his entire community.

"An fi de reason de smadi around wi now will. Fight to de death fah mi." He explained that's the reason the people that surrounded us, would fight to the death for him.

"And now, I will take you uptown to my home," he continued.

As we walked back to our vehicles, I was very impressed by the way people in Jamaica took authority into their own hands, to make sure that their entire communities survived. Regardless of how unfair they were treated.

Choyce and I got back into the SUV and were headed for uptown, to see how far being a blessing to others, would get you in the very heart of Kingston Jamaica.

*****

Black's mansion.

As we pulled up, I could see off top, how blessed Black was for doing the right thing by his people. Black's crib was not fenced, or gated, but walled in. It had a dual gated entry that led to a seven-thousand-square foot residence with front and back facades.

As we walked in the front door, Black had a

three-story foyer with a Romanesque fountain plaza. The mansion had a first, second, and third floor master suite. With ensuite bathrooms and a French elevator that went to all three levels of the house.

He had plenty of living and dining room space and inside and outside full basketball courts. Out back, he had a Romeo and Juliet staircase that had access to all three levels to the back of his house.

He had cabanas by the pool and a separate six-bedroom, seven full bath guesthouse. The most exclusive part to me was how the top master bedroom overlooked the Downtown area. I could see his garrison from up there.

"Damn, Choyce, you and I could be living like this right now," I commented.

"Yeah, if we packed up when we got home and came back," Choyce joked as we walked to pick out our rooms for the night.

"Nah, but for real, ah nigga can get used to this part of life," Choyce went on to say.

"Yeah, for a minute, I thought we were about to

sleep in a shack with some Israel Uzis around our necks and shit," I said and fell weak from laughter.

"Niggah, you just read my mind. I was going to sleep next to that ganja smoke and use a pound for a pillow. I already had with night figured out," Choyce joked back.

"What are you two in here laughing about?" Black questioned as he walked into the room.

"How we thought we had to sleep with Uzis around our necks and use pounds of ganja for pillows." Black must have known that's what we were thinking, by way he laughed with us. He passed us another blunt then left the room.

"Lil' bruh! Did you see how them females got to twerking hard as fuck as soon as they saw us?" Choyce questioned with excitement.

"Off top, bro, If I wasn't in a relationship, I would've been all over a couple of'em," I commented.

"Nah, for real. On everything, I gotta go back. Just to see this one girl. She was fine as fuck and crazy, stupid thick. I have to see if I can get her to twerk on this dick before we leave." Choyce got hyped about how them ladies twerked.

I couldn't stop thinking about Channy. I hadn't called her at all ever since we facetimed a couple weeks prior. I felt like I did her dirty. Just so the universe could honor my absence from her in my favor, I had to fall back from the Jamaican women. Although they did look beautiful and thick as fuck, I respected my queen even if she wasn't around.

Black texted Choyce and told us to come down. As we off elevator, we headed towards the pool area.

"What's good, Black, you wanted to see us?" Choyce questioned as we took a seat at his table.

"Mi just gat ah phone call fram fi mi garrison. And you got all the girls going crazy over you two," Black explained.

"An fi mi yardies ave mad Big Up fah aal of yuh two. And welcum yuh dem ah drow ah dance hall block party tenight." Black said that his gang had much respect for us and welcomed us to a dance hall block party that night.

"But before we go, let's eat, drink, and smoke on some high-grade ganja. Ah, dat cool wid unuh?" Black asked was that cool, and we were all for it.

"Hell, yeah it's cool with us," Choyce said.

"I told you they were feeling our vibe, lil' bruh," he rejoiced as we walked back to the elevator to go up to our rooms.

"Real recognize real everywhere on God's green earth," I commented.

As Choyce rambled on, I couldn't stop thinking about Channy. She'd been on my mind super tough. When got back, I had a lot of making up to do.

"I already know which one I want too, lil' bruh. As soon as she seen me, she turned around and made her ass jump so high, it high-fived a cloud," Choyce rejoiced as he rubbed his hands together.

"Bro, you're crazy, that shit was funny. Her ass high-fived a cloud, though?" I joked.

After we ate a good meal, we popped a few bottles, and smoked some more ganja. We got dressed, then met up with Black in the foyer by the front door.

*****

The dance hall block party.

The block party had been going on for a few hours before we even pulled up. So, as we're getting out the stretch Suburban, we were greeted by the full effect of what the dance hall culture is all about.

The genre of reggae music, crowds of people, and different styles of dancing were lit. Choyce and I were escorted through the crowd by a group of thugs and surrounded by gang of bad ass females. We followed them all through the block party.

"This is how it's supposed to be back home, Choyce. Instead of all that hating shit, they be on." Even Choyce couldn't help but embrace the moment.

I just felt blessed that we'd made it to see a day like that.

"Niggas ain't real, bro, they hated on us when they thought we didn't have shit. Now, they know we rich, that make them hate us even more. All I can say is look where moving smooth all these years got us!" Choyce explained as we shook up.

"Nah, for real. But fuck them haters, let's get lost in this moment," I agreed as we walked through the crowd. People showed us much love; we had females flocked around us and heavy security. Black led us toward the DJ booth then he grabbed the microphone.

"I want for you all to give it up for the real Kings of Indianapolis! Shu dem luv an let dem see de reaaaaal! Ou wi get dung har inna Kingston, Jamdung!" Black said as he told the masses to show us love and show us how they really got down in Kingston, Jamaica.

"Bad man Big up! Bad man! Murda mon dance Buck! Buck! Buck! Yuh haa mi now?" He said, "Show that gangster respect and murder man dance, you hear me now?"

The DJ spun a record that had everyone showing out. The scene was lit, all the ladies danced on me and my brother. They smelled good and looked very sexy.

"Lil' bruh, I told you she wanted me," Choyce nudged me and said. I saw what he meant; she twerked so hard on him, the way she threw her ass around. It could've given a high five to the clouds.

*****

5:30 a.m.

We were headed back to Blacks' crib with fifteen females, and they were all beautiful. We got out and went straight to the swimming pool. Choyce took the one he wanted, straight to his room. Black and I were in the jacuzzi with the rest.

"Right on Black, for showing me and my brother, the true definition of Jamrock," I said with a Cuban cigar in my mouth and two women under my arms.

"I have no problem with that, you look out for me and mine. An wi luk out fah yuh an fi yuh," Black said as he got his cigar and lit up.

"Off top, I'm just glad this is the favor we get in return. Jamaica is a beautiful place."

"Everything is alright when you come here. Ef fi mi smadi luv yuh. Den even ef im ded yuh always be welcome yah as ef fi mi duppy was standing rite nex to yuh." Black said if his people loved me, then even if he was dead, I'd always be welcome there as if his ghost was standing right next to me.

"I don't take that lightly and believe me, on behalf of Choyce and myself, it's an honor to have this exposure."

"We never been out of the country before, and you made this an experience to remember."

"Big up. I understand that you and your brother, had concerns about how I was able to ship all of those keys to you, right?"

"Yeah, I know you heard Choyce tell you he damn near didn't accept them." I laughed.

"We never seen nothing like it. We called you immediately," I continued to laugh and reached over to ash my cigar. I leaned my head and replayed that day in my mind.

"No, good. I have power ova de airport. If dey know dat it's fram mi de Babylon mon himself put a stamp on it." He said, he had power and as long as the drugs were from him, the policeman himself would put a stamp on it.

"Dey turn de x-ray machine off or dey know dat dem ah ded men walking." Black explained that if they tried to check what he sent out, they were dead men walking.

"Off top, but how did you get in power the way you are? That's a hell of ah influence you have, and you're not playing no games."

"Mi ah original Bad Man, an de Don Dada of mi garrison. Mi inna gud wid de Colombian an Mexican Cartel dey know mi pon ah first name basis."

He explained that he was an original gangster and the drug lord of his garrison. He was in good with the Colombian and the Mexican Cartel. They knew him on a first name basis.

"Mi sell kilos of crack to de Downtown, garrison dons. An mi sell kilos of coke. To de rich folk where we a now Uptown Hills." He said that he sold kilos of crack to the Downtown garrison dons. And sold kilos of coke to the rich folk, where he lived in the Uptown Hills.

"Real niggas do real things, Black. My brother I are glad to be a part of it," I said out of respect.

Ever since I was a kid, I'd soaked up the game. I

always kept a close eye on Choyce; I never said a word just listened to him. He taught me everything he knew. I witnessed Choyce excel in the street life. So, I believed Black's story.

"Nuh doubt but mi ave som Colombians. Coming up inna few days unexpectedly. Mi affi see ou dis ah guh fi guh." Black told me his Colombian connect would be up in a few days, and I had to see how it was going to go.

"Guh suh in sending yuh an fi yuh broder, to Montego Bay fi de rest of fi yuh tan pon. Call mi wen yuh mek it bakka yawd. An ill will send yuh something bigga. An it should lass fah ah lon while."

Black went on to say that he was sending me and Choyce, to stay in Montego Bay for the rest of our stay--on him. He wanted us to call him when we made it back home, and he would send us something that was bigger than the last time. He said that should last us for a long while.

"Say less, and I'll make sure to let Choyce knows the game plan. And thank you once again." I was drunk and high, so two of the ladies helped me out of the jacuzzi led me to my room.

Montego Bay

After we took a swim, I told Choyce everything Black and I had discussed. We stood on the shore as we overlooked the Caribbean Sea. We were surrounded by cliffs, sandy beaches, and water.

"Chance, tell me the truth. Did you fuck them bitches that was in your room, this morning?" Choyce questioned and gave me the stare down with one eyebrow raised.

"Hell nah, I was drunk and high as fuck, but couldn't stop thinking about Channy," I said as looked out into the sea as if I could see her walking on the water right toward me.

"Well, I fucked the shit out of Meka, my lil' bruh. She was trying to take it, but I had her in total submission when it was all said and done," Choyce bragged as he motioned like he beat her pussy up.

"Did you use a condom, bro?" I asked then gave him the stare down.

"Off top, I had to, I'm trying to raise a family one day. I can't throw it all away on one night's pleasure," Choyce said and acted as if he'd shot a three-pointer into the sea.

"What you think about college, Chance? I mean, I know you aren't thinking about giving up on your dream, are you?" bro questioned out of the blue.

"I'll have to see after this surgery. I mean, it feels like I'm healing, I'm just not trying to get my heart broke if the surgery doesn't work," I answered.

"Heart broke for what? Bro, you're an academic scholar that graduated head of our class. I know you had your heart set on the NFL. But what's plan B?" Choyce questioned as he gave his heart-to-heart.

"I know there's more out here, but I trained hard to get to that University. I'm not going to give up, but like I said, I'll have to make my next move after this surgery," I said as I tried to rotate my arm and could still feel the pain. It didn't hurt as bad as it used to though.

"I wouldn't be able to attend until the spring semester, next year anyway. My surgery is scheduled too far out," I stressed my concern.

"Well, lil' bruh, if all else fails, we got money already. I'm talking M's apiece, early. We did it, bro, so don't feel to down, however it works out," bro assured as he put his arm around my shoulder.

"But on some other shit, I'm thinking about starting a family, lil' bruh." That was the second time Choyce had made that statement. I just thought that swim in the sea made him delirious.

"Okay, I get it. You done fell in love, bro!" I laughed hard.

"Man, hell no, I'm not in love," Choyce commented as if he were embarrassed

"Bro, I'm the last person you can lie to. We're twins, there's nothing you can hide from me. I know you like a book!" I laughed even harder.

"Let me guess, it's Unique, isn't it?" I questioned and looked over as I awaited my answer.

"Man, yelp."

"I knew it, bro. Y'all been spending way too much time together, for you not to have feelings for her."

"We aren't kid's anymore, lil' bruh. We got a whole 'nother legacy besides ours to leave out here." I was impressed, the player of all players, himself wanted to settle down.

I let the conversation end on that note. Choyce had a change of heart. I supported that, and that made me decide to go back to school. Just like mom told me and bro a long time ago. Warning comes before destruction.

Chapter 4

We landed at the airport, but as we were landing, I saw like fifteen police cars parked. I thought nothing of it. Choyce had to use the restroom while I stood in baggage claim. I saw six officers headed my way. I didn't know why, but I was nervous as fuck. Before I knew, it two of them pointed directly at me.

"Chance Coleman, I'm going to need for you to put your hands behind your back. Once we securely place these hand cuffs on you, then you will be coming with us." I had no idea what I'd done.

"What's this about?" I questioned as they placed me in handcuffs.

"What the fuck y'all doing to my brother!" Choyce yelled as he aggressively walked towards us.

"Get the fuck back!" an officer yelled as five more rushed over.

"Nah, fuck getting back, let my brother the fuck go!" Choyce demanded.

"I'm telling you one more time to get the fuck

back! Or I'll lock you up for intimidation!" Choyce didn't give a fuck, he shoved his way through the officers, and they attacked him and held him down, but he didn't get arrested though.

"Get the fuck off me!" I yelled! I put up a struggle, but I was thrown to the ground.

"We got Ricky and we're coming for Doughboy next," an officer sarcastically stated, then they all laughed as they picked me off the ground and took me straight to county jail.

*****

They sat me in an investigation room. I looked at the door knob the entire time. When I saw it twist, my heart dropped to the bottom of my feet.

"Well, Mr. Coleman, we finally caught up with you," the detective said as he entered the room and took a seat across the table from me.

"What the fuck was you trying to catch up with me for? I hadn't done anything?" I answered. I was lost as to what I'd done. It was so wrong they had to arrest me at the airport.

"Well, let me say this, first. I heard a lot about you. I heard about your football career and that your life was great. At what point did your life take a turn for the worst, and I want for you to start me off at that turning point," he said as he placed a recorder on the table and was about to press play.

"I have no idea about any wrong turns and shit like that. I have nothing to say about anything. I know my rights, and I would like to speak with my attorney," I said as I looked off to the side, ready for whatever was next.

"Well, let me tell you this now, a couple eyewitnesses placed you at a shooting that led to an homicide a couple weeks ago, but I don't think you're the one who pulled the trigger," the detective said as he sat back in his chair.

When he mentioned I was wanted for a shooting tied to a homicide, my entire life flashed before my eyes. I thought I was done for, no longer able to accomplish my dreams.

"Now, we can do this easy way, and you give up your brother. Or we can do this the hard way and you catch your fist murder case for him, right now," he stated.

"Before you answer, think about your football career. I honestly don't believe you did it. I'm on your side, so just give your brother up because you have a lot more to lose than he does," he finished talking then pressed record.

"I don't know shit and don't got shit for you. So, fuck what you're talking about and do what you have to do," I answered.

"Ok, have it your way. Stand to your feet, you're under arrest for murder. We know for a fact it was your brother. So, either tell me what you know or sit in the county until your court date."

"Sir, I have no idea what you are talking about. I'm not about to answer any questions about a murder or nothing, now take me wherever. Like I said, I want to talk to my attorney."

*****

"Chow time!" I heard someone yell and woke me up the next morning.

I didn't even remember falling asleep. I looked

around, and I was in an orange jump suit, laid on a bottom bunk in a jail cell.

"Man, fuck!" I yelled. I had already made my call to Choyce. He told me he had already made my bond, but they had a seventy-two-hour hold on me.

I walked out my cell and grabbed my breakfast tray. I sat at one of the tables across from the TV, and my face was broadcasted all over it with a caption.

Breaking news: Number one running back in the nation charged for murder.

I was disgusted and slid my tray forward. I couldn't eat that nasty ass food if I wanted to.

"Just the nigga I've been waiting to see," someone said as he sat next me.

"The fuck? Why were you waiting to see me, do I know you?" I questioned as I mean-mugged dude.

"I'm KB. Look, I got some very information for you. It's going to cost you, though," he explained.

"Talk to me, KB. What's good?" I questioned.

He had one of them grimy vibes about him, and I knew I couldn't trust him. So, I kept my conversation limited.

"Look, I was there the day you or your bitch ass brother killed my nigga, Delyn. The police locked me and my nigga up a couple days later," KB said as he scooted closer and aggressively talked by my ear.

"We decided make our statements on you because we knew you were the more pussy one. He got out already, but I had priors, so I got a high ass bond. Look, if you want us to keep our mouths shut, you'd better do as I say, fuck nigga. Or I can stab you the fuck up right now," he threatened as he exposed a small knife then held it by my side.

I was nervous, but I had to keep my composure. One thing my dad taught me was never let another man see you sweat.

"Fuck you, nigga, I don't know about no murder or none of that shit. But since I do know what you want, I'll make a call once I make bond, and we can talk then." I saw the greed in his eyes, and I knew how to go about his type.

"That's coo, but I'm ah need a couple of them

keys from you too. Or I'll make my statement official. If you don't come through on your end, I'll make sure that it sticks. You feel me?" he questioned as he stood to walk away, but I stopped him.

"Write your full name down, bro. I don't know what the fuck you're talking about, but I can get you home."

*****

One week later.

Once I was released, I made good on my promise. I called Mr. McFarland, and he got KB bailed out. Before I left, I gave him my number and told him to call me when they released him.

I didn't tell Choyce because of the way KB threatened my life. I just felt it was personal, and that bitch as nigga had no idea, what I was going through. So, I had to play it cool, until I had him and his snitching ass partner together and end them both.

I sat in my car, Downtown across the street from the county jail as I waited on KB to come out. It had been cloudy all day, like it was going to rain. I saw someone come out of the county jail and cross the street. He headed to my passenger side window. He knocked on it, so I let it down.

"Aye, Chance, let me hallah at you right quick," he said as he bent to look in my car.

"What's up?" I questioned and tried to get a good look at thug, but I didn't know him.

"You're here to pick up KB, right?" he asked and looked around.

"Yeah, but speak up, you are asking too many questions." I was upset he kept beating around the bush and wouldn't tell me shit.

"Look, my name is James, but people call me JR. I'm just trying to let you know that when you got released, that nigga KB was in that mufuckah trippin out," he said.

"I know, the nigga was buggin while I was in there. Talkin bout the police were asking about me and shit. Get in it right quick, JR, it's about to start raining." After he finally stated his business, I knew to let him in. I could see that God had sent him my way.

"Yeah, my nigga, this is crazy that I just got released. But I got moved to the same cell you was in after you bonded out," he explained.

"My right hand to the Lord, he woke on some bullshit. He told me he and his guy got pulled over with them two keys you threw on the ground, the day of the shootout. If you didn't bond him out and give him whatever he asked for, he would personally make sure that he testified on you."

"Chance, the whole city knows about you and your brother. If you're looking for a soldier to get him out of here, then hell, put me down. Because that nigga is on some bullshit," JR offered.

"Nah, for real? But I got you, how much are you looking for to make it happen, my nigga?" I questioned, just to see where his heart was at.

"Man, I'll do the shit for free. You and your brother are out here all major and shit. If that's what I'll have to do to prove myself to you, then like I said, I'll get him all the way together for the free."

As I looked at JR. He looked like one of them

loyal cut-throat mufuckahs, I needed for the job.

"Were you from, bro?" I asked just to see if we had a house on his side of town. After he did that for me, I was going to put him on.

"I'm from the Barrington Projects out south. I'm under Dave the Southside Don. It's just that I'm fucked up right now because he's in the joint."

"He was ah real nigga like you are. He got told on by a fuck nigga like KB. And Dave is gone for good because of it."

"But you're too real, to have some hoe ass shit like that happen to you. Here's my number. Call me because here comes that hoe ass nigga leaving out of the county now," he said as we looked over and saw KB walking out the front door.

"I'm ah hit your line in ah minute, good looking out."

"No doubt, real recognizes real." As JR got out of the car, KB had just walked up to the door. JR mean mugged the shit out of him as KB got in. JR just put his hood on his head and walked off.

"You know that dude, KB?" I asked just to see how dependable JR's information was.

"Yeah, we were in the same block. He just got out right before I did," he said as he shut the door and laid his seat back.

"So, about that statement, I can have you and your guy in a good position if you two can keep your mouths shut," I said as I put the car in drive and drove off.

"Do that, I really want blood for my nigga, Delyn. But since you're ready to comply to my demands, I'll let you live. How long is it going to take?" he questioned as he looked over at me.

"Thank you for sparing me, I felt like you gave me a second chance at life. So, I gotta make it right by you and your guy. Just give me a few days to get it together for you, and we should be straight," I replied.

I was just playing my role because I didn't have both them in the same place. I had to put together a plan that would kill two birds with one stone.

"Nah, fuck a couple days, nigga! I need that

shit, asap. I'll jump out this bitch right now and go give my statement," he said as he reached for the door handle. We were just a few blocks up, so I had to make a quick decision.

"Look, what good is two kilos, when you can get five? Call your guy, tell him that I'm willing to give you each five keys to split. And one-hundred bands apiece to keep your mouths shut," I offered. He fed into my fear, and I knew his greed wouldn't let him refuse the offer.

"Okay, now we're on the same page. Shit, drop me off at my mom's house. I'll call my guy, and I'll hit you up around 10:30 when we're ready," he replied just like I thought he would.

*****

I dropped him off, then headed to a park not too far from my hood. I had to chill out for a minute. I was so stressed out, I had to roll up a blunt. After I finished, I let my seat back as I faced my blunt and thought over my life."

I had to tighten up my grip, and iron-fist on them niggah because how they tried to hoe me. I had to kill them niggas because they had my entire future in the palms of their greedy ass hands. I'd said fuck it and put these fuck nigga's demise into motion.

I was going to take them to one of the houses, but that would've tied them to me. So, I remembered a house that Choyce and I were going to buy. When we went to check it out, the door was unlocked, and the lights were on. It was too many holes in the walls and flooded bad. So, we passed it up.

So, I went to the warehouse got five keys and two-hundred bands. When I pulled up to the house, it was still vacant. The door was locked, but the window was cracked, and it still had power. I could tell people had been there to remodel it because of all drywall, paint buckets, and cleaning supplies. I staged my play then made my calls.

*****

"What's up, who diss?"

"What's up, JR. this is Chance."

"Oh, shit what's up foo? I've been waiting for you to call all day. So, am I on the team, my nigga?" he questioned and sounded hungry.

"Nah, but I got twenty bands for two heads type of shit," I answered.

"With money like that, you don't need to be on anybody's team. You can be your own boss, but I'll keep you plugged on that good coke though. That's the best I can do."

"Nah, fuck that. I'll get them gone for da free, my niggah. Just to show you how solid I really am." He wouldn't take no for answer, but I couldn't let that be a free mission because then, he might've thought I owed him in the long run.

"No, nigga, listen! You should already know by now, that the only time you turn down bands is when someone tries to hand them to you for free! Don't trust that shit, JR, believe me. It will be better if you get paid for this work you about to put in. Fuck free, take the money."

"I feel that I'm just trying to show you my loyalty, that's all."

"I feel you, but loyalty isn't free. I'm sending you

in on a mission, my nigga, you about to take something that don't belong to you or me. Don't walk away empty-handed. No favors, my nigga, remember that," I addressed with aggression.

"Don't ever let ah nigga make you feel like you need them. Work hard play hard out here and fuck all that partying bullshit in the process of it. That's what these two fuck-niggas is about to get wacked for right now," I finished.

"Real shit, Chance, put me up on game. I see why real niggas respect you. Any other nigga would have let me do the shit, but you're saying, I would've felt you owed me later if I get fucked up," he agreed.

"By you breaking bread with me, right now, that makes us partners and shit. I get it, say no more, I'm ready when you are."

JR understood what I was saying. Some niggas were so ready to please the next man, that they forgot about themselves. When they got locked up or went broke, all their inner demons tormented them for the sins they did for free. Those demons screamed out night and day in their minds--*Pay me!*

When one couldn't meet their own demon's demands, that type of stress could cause a solid nigga to turn into a venomous snake. That's the type of shit I was going through with KB and his guy.

"Nah, for real. Meet me at 2918 Ruckle Street. It's right off the corner of 29th."

"What time, bro?"

"10:30."

*****

I went to pick up KB and guy, and those niggas, didn't have the sense that God gave them.

"Chance, you better be lucky you came through for us. We had your number, fuck nigga," KB said as a threat, and I could just feel their jealous, vexed spirts all in my car.

"Man, fuck this nigga! Why we gotta ride with you anyway? He might be trying to set us up! Show us those two bricks, nigga! Or I'll end you right now!" his guy yelled out and cocked his gun.

I had to think quick, those niggas were hungry.

But I knew their greed was their downfall.

"Wait a minute, I made a deal for one-hundred bands apiece, and five keys for y'all to split. I wasn't about to ride with all that on me. I just heard you say two keys so, I take it KB hasn't run that past you, yet?" I had to play a game of psychological warfare with those niggas, use their greed to turn them against each other before they killed me.

"Nah, KB, you didn't tell me that part. What's that about, nigga?" dude questioned.

I could then feel all the tension avert from me onto KB.

"My bad, I meant to tell you, but it slipped my mind. I'm glad you brought that up though, Chance."

They both got quiet as we turned on to the street. Choyce always told me that birds of a feather flocked together, and snitches came in pairs. As we pulled up, it was dark as hell on that block like somebody shot out the streetlights.

I told JR the door was unlocked and to just hide in a room until I left.

"Why the fuck is it so dark? Chance, I'm telling you; this better not be a set up," KB said and pulled out his gun as we parked in front of the house.

"Nah, I'm a man of my word. Those bands and keys are in the house." KB snatched my car key and put his gun to my head.

"Let's go," he ordered. We all got out and went up to the house, but I stopped when I got to the door. What if JR played me and was in on that with them?

I got nervous. I just hoped JR was solid and didn't take that shit for himself. After all, it was two-hundred bands and five keys of coke. I had them laid out in the middle of the floor of the front room because I knew it might've come down to that. So, I had to make it seem like I played my part.

"Open the door, nigga!" KB's guy demanded. As soon as I did, they saw what they were looking for.

"Damn, KB, I still can't believe you wasn't about to tell me this part," his guy said then pointed his gun at KB.

"The fuck is you doing? I was going to tell you,

but it slipped my mind!" KB yelled in his defense. He then pointed his gun back at his partner.

"Nigga, you know damn well ain't no bullets in that gun! You influenced me to snitch on this nigga just to get yo bitch ass out of trouble! Got my name all fucked up in these streets, and you were trying to keep this from me!" Before I know it, dude pulled his trigger. KB flew back into the wall.

JR was in the closet with the door cracked, right by the light switch. I knew I was next, so I nodded my head, and JR flipped the switch.

"What the fuck!" dude yelled out. I dove to the floor. It was a five second shootout, and then the light came back on.

"Chance, you good, my nigga?" JR questioned. When I looked up, he had blood seeping through the side of his shirt.

"Yeah, I'm straight, are you?" I questioned as I looked at his side. He looked down then pulled up his shirt.

"Damn, I got grazed. Nigga, this shit hurt bad

than ah bitch!" he answered. I looked around and saw a few cleaning supplies.

"Use these rags, bro, clean off everything you touched. Wrap that sheet around your side, make sure you're not dripping any more blood. My nigga, you got two-hundred bands and five keys. Ain't no looking back from here. Give me your phone," I said as I collected KB and his guy's cell phones and my car key.

I helped JR clean up. I used a flat head screwdriver to get the bullet out the wall with his blood on it. JR took a hammer to knock out the drywall it was lodged in. That side of the wall was still fucked up any way.

I took the gun KB had and wiped off then put JR's gun in KB's hand. After we moved KB's body by the closet, I used KB's finger to pull the trigger a couple times, then I was ready to get the fuck out of there.

"Just don't get caught, my nigga," I said as I left the house.

The rest was up to him.

*****

August 23rd *3:30 a.m.*

I was once again laid in my room, sleepless with a mind full of worries. I didn't know if my plan worked or not. On top of all my other troubles, I had to my put anxieties on hold because I had to reach out to Channy. It was going on two months, and I hadn't called or nothing.

I reached in my drawer to get my other phone out. As soon as I powered it on, it was like it was possessed. It dinged with so many notifications and missed calls that my phone locked up.

I had to call her from my other phone.

"Hello, babe. Look, I just wanna say—"

"Fuck you, Chance!" she screamed right before I could go into my sob story.

"Damn, hello?" I questioned.

"You're full of shit! Just like all these other fuck niggah!" She was serious than ah mufuckah, and she had me nervous as fuck. I stood in the middle of my bedroom in nothing but my draws.

"Yeah, nigga! You can run, but you can't hide!

When I catch up with you and that other bitch! I'm ah kill both you mufuckahs!" she threatened and cocked a gun.

Every time I tried to explain, she cut me off.

"Fuck you! You bitch ass nigga…. you're….full…of…shit. And I'm ah chop your dick off!" She went so hard, I just wanted to hang up.

"I'm mean, what other bitch, I'm confused?"

"Yeah nigga, be dat, protect that bitch if you want to! But I got something that will confuse your lying ass even more! Fuck nigga, I'm pregnant. Now, tell that bitch you're about to be a father, nigga! What you got to say about that, with your stupid ass?"

I was speechless. I saw why she was on mind so much. I knew it was deeper than the love I had for her. She was pregnant with my child. I had mixed emotions; I had an entire murder case that hung over my head. It didn't know what to do.

"Babe, can I talk, please? I didn't' reach out because I was going through a lot of shit. I'm happy you're pregnant. I'm about to be a father, but please, I know it's hard to believe. There is no other woman. Once again, you are all I know," I explained, but I still felt like I didn't get through to her.

"Why aren't you at school, babe? The semester already started," I questioned.

"Because you're not there, plus, I found out I was pregnant a month ago. I couldn't tell you, because you were nowhere to be found, and fuck you, Chance." She didn't even breathe to get that out so, I had let me calm her down.

"Channy, stop crying. I'm sorry, I had a lot going on, plus Choyce and I took a trip out of the country. I promised myself that I was going to call you when I got back, but I got locked up at the airport. It's all my fault. I'm sorry, and I love you."

"Yeah, you ah sorry ass nigga. So, where did you go out of the country with your no-good, lying ass? And what did you get locked up for? You know you can't play football with felonies, stupid?" I could tell that she rolled her neck the whole time she talked.

"We took a business trip to Jamaica, and I thought about you the entire time. I even bought you a gift back. Don't worry about me getting locked up, they had the wrong person, and the charge won't stick," I explained. I had to lie about the gift to throw her off, but since she told me she was pregnant, I had something even better in stored for her.

"Okay, because I know my babe didn't do nothing wrong, and what did you bring me back?" she questioned.

"You will have to come see, or I'll bring it to you."

"Well, I got into a car accident tripping out over you. So, you're going to have to come see me."

"Damn, are you alright?"

"No!"

"Well, what happened?"

"I lost my G-Wagon, that's what happened. I had my seat belt on, and air bag deployed properly, so I'm ight."

"Well, I got insurance, so you'll be back on the road in no time. I'm on my way, so be looking out for me."

"Okay, zaddy."

August 26th

It was Choyce and my nineteenth birthday, and we'd planned a big ass birthday party at our club. We sat in our office early in the morning to discuss a few things before we started our day.

"I talked to Tory. He said the witnesses to your case, shot and killed each other. He also told me you gave him money to hire a bail bondsman to get one of'em out," Choyce said. He leaned back in his chair then looked over at me.

"So, what does that mean, now?" I questioned. That was the first time, I'd ever been in a situation like that. I only followed my instincts and did what I had to do.

"They don't have a case now, but when I found out where it happened at, I remembered us looking into that buying that house. Once I put two and two together, you just don't know how mad I was at you. Why did you keep that shit to yourself? Lil' bruh, you know you could've come to me. I would've taken care of it for you," Choyce expressed his concern.

"Nah, bro. That was personal, those niggas were on some bullshit with me. They tried to come between me and my dreams, over some greedy shit. One of them threatened to stab me in the county. They thought I was sweet, I had to show them, bro," I explained, not expecting anyone to ever understand.

"Nah, for real. Lil' bruh, that was some good shit. Troy didn't go through the same bail bondsman he did for you, so you can't be linked all the way around. You're a smart hood nigga for the play you put down. Don't trip, I took care of the rest of them niggas while you were locked up in the county," Choyce said as he leaned forward and looked puzzled.

"I still don't know how you got them niggas to kill each other. That was some mastermind next level shit. I ain't ever pulled no shit off like that. But thank you for keeping it solid with me too. I knew you wouldn't, but you didn't fold on me. We good now because of it, let's get ready for this B-day, lil' bruh. We deserve this shit."

Chapter 5

Channy had no idea, but I had a part of our birthday, set up completely around her.

"Lil' bruh, I got word that we still, got some opp ass niggas on that fuck shit wit us. So, I beefed up security tonight. We shouldn't have no problems, but we got all the guns in the upstairs VIP," Choyce said as he came into my room.

"Off top, bro. But fuck that, I got something special planned for Channy at the lower level. She is carrying my seed, so tonight, I'm ah make it official," I said as I looked at myself in the mirror.

I had on a red Christian Dior button-up, with the dress pants and the loafers to match. Choyce saw how fresh I was going to be and had to follow suit, he came with the all-gold Christian Dior button-up, pants, and loafers.

"Nah, for real? That's what we're on then, congratulations once again. I'm ready whenever you are.

"Off, top. I'll be ready in a second," I said as I

applied my drip.

Choyce got in touch with Black; he had his brother take over the jewelry side of their business. That's how his family moved up rank. He was the next to don in their garrison. Choyce had us two crowns made, one white gold to go with my drip, and one all gold to go with his.

I placed my order and had on a custom diamond Rolex Datejust 41 watch, with the two-tone red Arabic numerals. My chain had the two-tone red diamonds in it, with the ring to go with it. That shit hit hard with my crown, but the gift I got for Channy was what impressed me the most.

*****

We walked into our club, to Lil Tjay's song *Zoo York* featuring *Fivio Foreign* and *Pop Smoke*. We and that bitch lit as we were greeted by the crowed. I let bro do the set up, and he had some wild idea, he had to get out his system. He had stripper poles throughout the entire club. He hired almost every stripper in the city to come out.

Although we were under-aged, we didn't let anyone under twenty-one in, half the people our age was on that fuck shit anyway. Choyce had Muhammed rent out the club for the night and, he had his liquor licenses and all. Once again, we bought the entire city out. Choyce had us two thrones that sat in the upstairs VIP, and I had two put downstairs for later.

After we made our appearance, I went straight to my office. I was nervous as fuck and I practiced my proposal repeatedly and still couldn't get it right.

"Lil' bruh! Why the fuck is you in here sweating bullets and shit?" Choyce questioned as he busted into our office and laughed.

"Shit, bro, I can't remember what I wanted to say. I'm about to say fuck it. She doesn't know I'm about to do it anyway," I said as I closed the ring box back.

"Well, you study long, you study wrong, pimp. Your queen has arrived," he said then pointed downstairs. Bro made sure he had heavy security escort her and her entourage to the elevator.

She was on her way up, so I grabbed my sweat

towel and got myself together. I stood by the elevator. Once the door opened, I was amazed. She was beyond beautiful, I told her I was wearing all Christian Dior. So, she made she sure she matched my fly.

She had her hair in a long ponytail that came down to the middle of her back. Her makeup, nails, and toes matched perfectly with the colors she had on. I could smell her before, she even walked up on me.

She was wearing a short, red spaghetti strapped dress with the sides cut low around her hips but covered her ass properly. The front showed off the right amount of her boobs and a part of her stomach with some nice red bottoms. She had on a white gold diamond choker with a pretty bracelet and watch. All she was missing, was the ring I had for her.

"Babe, you look beautiful" I said as I reached for a hug.

"Don't 'babe' me, I should smack the fuck out you," she said. Before I could respond, she kissed me on my lips.

"Happy birthday, babe. You look gorgeous,

king. Besides the crown, I know you ain't dripping this hard and didn't get me nothing?" she questioned then handed me my gift.

"How could I forget about my queen?" I answered then kissed her again.

I pulled her close and hugged her tightly. I found myself not knowing what to do without her. I needed her in my life until I was no more.

"This is real nice, Chance. Y'all went all out this. I love it. Happy birthday, again," Channy said as she sat on my lap and hit her blunt a few times then passed it to me.

Choyce and Unique got into an argument because he'd hired all those strippers. He took her in the office, and I already knew what they started to do. Channy and I just laughed.

It was one a.m., and I had the party stopped. Security rolled out his and hers thrones, then placed them in the middle of the dance floor.

"What the fuck is going on?" Channy questioned.

"Are you two ready?" security asked as they surround us.

"Come on, babe," I said. I stood to my feet and took her by the hand. I had her a crown made too, and it was the more feminine version of mine.

"Where are we going, babe?" Channy questioned once again. One of my security had her crown on a silk pillow. When she turned around and saw it, tears filled her eyes. She loved it.

"Oh, my God. Chance, will you please tell me what's going on?" she asked as he placed the crown on her head.

"Just follow me, babe, it will all make since in a second, trust me." We got escorted to the elevator. As we stood side by side, I could see tears of joy stream down her face.

We got off the elevator, and I walked her to her throne. I helped her sit down, but I got down one knee.

"Chance, is this what I think it is?" she questioned. As so many tears streamed down her face, she fanned herself.

"You told me to promise you forever. Well, here it is. I love you more than life itself. I had an entire speech, but I'm so nervous, I forgot," I said as I pulled out the ring box from my back pocket and opened it. I got her a custom made seven-karat Asscher Cut Octavia diamond engagement ring.

"Babe, you ain't gotta say shit! That ring is speaking for itself, just ask the question and put it on meh!" she yelled out. Once again, her humor had not only me but everyone around us in tears from laughter.

"Channy Nycole, will you marry me?" I questioned as I took the ring out the box and tossed it to the side.

"Yes, Chance! Yes, I'll marry you, babe!" she agreed as she stomped her feet and wiggled her fingers until I placed the ring on.

"Boom! Bitches, he's all mine until he fucks up and I kill his ass, now what!" she joked as she held the ring up for all to see.

She had everyone weak as fuck, I didn't see what was so funny though. I wrapped my arms around her, and we kissed to seal the deal. The DJ tuned back up, and we got escorted back upstairs.

We received nothing but love with the congratulations. Choyce and Unique had settled their differences and were right there as soon as we stepped off the elevator. Unique rushed off to the side with Channy while Choyce and I shook up and sat back down on our thrones.

*****

Choyce and I sat in our office after everyone left. We discussed the direction our lives were headed, over a fifth of D'usse, with our feet up on our office desk.

"Choyce, you know our money, is getting to outrageous again. I think it's time to do another count up," I said.

I looked at him with a grin on my face because after the first time we tried it, he'd seem to a nervous breakdown if he heard the word count.

"What the fuck?" he said and almost fell backwards out of his chair.

"Bro, don't tell me that, the thought of counting

money makes your nervous, now." I laughed.

"Niggah I don't even give a fuck no more. We got money, and that's all that matters," he stated as if he'd ever seen another money counter, he'd shoot the shit out of it.

"This shit is crazy for real. Who would've ever thought that we would be millionaires at the ages of nineteen?" I questioned, then thought back on our journey.

"I did, I'm just shitty Justin isn't here to see this day," Choyce said as he poured himself another shot.

"Shiid, long live Justin, bro," I said as I poured myself a shot, and we did a toast.

"Congratulations, once again, bro. I'm proud of you. My lil' bruh's about to start a family!" Choyce rejoiced.

"Off top. Bro, thank you, man. This means a lot coming from you," I said as we shook up.

"Nah, for real. But let me just say this, Chance, I almost lost you three times. Once due to a kidnapping, when you got shot, and with this recent murder case scare," Choyce said as he stood in front of me, to look me eye to eye.

"Although you and I are rich, money can't replace what you mean to me. When I see you, all I can see is my lil' bruh. The one who used to carry a football around everywhere you went, with your hat to the back, and no shirt on." He laughed.

"I'll go to hell and back for you, lil' bruh, this game I play is ah mufuckah. It's a lot that comes with this, but you and I take to life's changes, just like fish do when currents shift. No matter who we wanted to grow up to be, we was, who we was before we got here," Choyce said as he walked over and took a seat in his chair.

I understood what he was saying, although I had my heart set on football. If I would've squared up and let Choyce choose his path while I chose mine, no one would've been there to help him change his path.

I had to be there for him, that was my twin brother. They say, "Born alone, die alone." Well, he was only five minutes older than me, and he needed me as much as I needed him. If he were in the streets wasting his time, I would've been stopped fuckin with him. He was just one of them ones though. The one who took you front seat on a wild roller coaster but knew how to navigate every twist, turn, and curve. Once it was over, you'd say, "I was there the entire ride."

"I love you, bro. You showed me how to survive out here, But I got to get back to my dreams. I got in touch with my coach, he caught wind of my murder allegation. Once he found out it had nothing to do with me, I got my scholarship back."

"He knew about me getting shot and wanted me to heal up. So, I got one more year before I head off to college.

"My surgery is in October, until then, let's keep this shit going, bro. I just gotta make sure you got everything in order, before I move on. How long do you plan to do this shit?" I questioned with concern.

"To tell you the truth, Unique and I are in the process of opening up our own real estate agency. I'm naming it *His and Hers Real Estate INC*. I just paid for her realtor classes."

"I figure if she was persuasive enough to talk me out of being a player, she could sell salt to a snail," he said as we laughed hard.

"Off top, bro, that's the move right there. I saw how she was on your top, too. Nigga, that was the first time, I ever saw a female put you in check." I laughed.

"Yeah, you saw me take her straight in here though, right? By the way, you may not wanna sit right there," he said as I jumped up out my seat.

"I'm just bullshitting, lil' burh. I did bang the shit out of her on the office desk, though."

"Nah, but once you go back to school, I'm ah get my realtor's license as well. I can't have you to worried about me while you're away," Choyce said as we left the office. Channy had just texted me to let me know, she was ready anyway.

Chapter 6

Channy told me, her mom wanted to talk with me. I kinda figured that, so I turned down my shine down to present that *I'm the father of your daughter's baby* image.

Channy was already outside when I pulled up. I got out, and we hugged and kissed. She walked me to the front door, then used her arm and foot to block me out.

"What did I do, now?" I asked, ready to listen, so I could correct the problem.

"Nothing. Nothing at all, but I want a house." She gave me a look like what she said wasn't up for discussion.

"I got plenty of rental properties, you don't want to move in one of them?" I questioned. Choyce and I had plenty of money invested into them. They were some nice homes, but she didn't seem to care about none of that.

"Nope, I'm ah need for you to stop being so cheap and break bread or play dead, nigga." Channy said with an unimpressed look on her face and had my back against the wall.

"I'm talking about a house, house, a big home somewhere way far away," she said and wouldn't move out of the way. Which gave me the impression that if I didn't give her what she wanted, then she was going in the house, and the door would slam in my face.

"Where did you have in mind, babe?" I questioned and felt a little under pressure.

"I was thinking out east in the Warren Township area, but that's kind of far, don't you think?"

"Nah, that's just a hop, skip, and a jump from the hood." I laughed.

"I thought you were talking about Alaska or something. What kind of homes are out that way anyway?"

"I'm glad you asked, we have a meeting with a lady named Mrs. Karen Lons tomorrow at noon. So, we can go from there," Channy said, then took her hand and foot from out of the doorway.

As I took a step forward, she quickly placed them back.

"I didn't hear an answer?"

"Alright, we can check it out," I answered. She smiled and finally let me in. I couldn't help but notice she'd been coached the whole time. When her mom saw me, she walked into the kitchen, and I could see her grin as if to say.

"That's my daughter."

After I spoke with Channy and her mom, I had to leave and hook up with Choyce, so I could get a little coaching myself.

*****

"What's good, bro?" I questioned as I walked into his room.

"Not shit, I got a lot on my mind right now, just trying to line all my ducks in a row," he said as he sat on the edge of his bed.

"What's up, though, lil' bruh. What's on your mind?" Choyce asked and looked drained from multitasking day in and out.

"Channy wants for me to buy us a big house. Being that we are our own financial advisors, I wanted to know how much money I should spend without getting a red flagged by the IRS?" I just didn't want to go all out on buying a home and get Choyce and I fucked up in the long run.

"We got a lot of houses that are suitable for your family, she doesn't want to live in one of them?"

"Nah, big bro I tried that, and she called it the cheap way." I laughed.

"Nah, for real. Now that I think about it, she's right, and I'm glad that you consulted with me first. Does she know what side of town she wanted to stay on? I'm assuming she wants to stay here in the city. Right?" he questioned as if it weren't me leaving the city for college and moving out of town wasn't an option.

"Yeah, she wants to stay here, but head far east in the Warren Township area," I assured.

"Okay, that area has some nice houses. But five-hundred thousand will keep you under the radar. Once you buy it, you can make as many changes to the inside as you want," Choyce advised and had all my attention.

"But five-hundred bands should be enough to get started on your first home together. After you upgrade it and it raises in equity, we could then put it on the market, sell it, and get you to something bigger." Choyce had me impressed; he sounded like a professional realtor.

"That would be a good opportunity to put our construction company to use," Choyce suggested.

"Off top, say less. We got a meeting with the homeowners, tomorrow, and I'm just going to have to get that house for her," I said as I stared off into space. Choyce just busted out laughing.

"Lil' bruh! You look like she got you by the balls this time. I haven't ever seen you stare off in space like this. What they say? Ah happy wife, happy life," he joked.

"Hell, yeah, bro. She put it on me this morning. Once we get this house, I'm going to get my man cave started quickly."

"Good, now I can remodel this house since I'm the only one left. I'm about to flip the fuck out of it.

*****

We pulled up to the address and parked in front of the residence. Channy and I got out of our car.

"Oh, my God. Chance, look at this house, it's so beautiful from out here. I can't wait to see the inside of it," Channy expressed how happy she was about the situation.

"You like it?" I asked.

I hoped we didn't have to house hunt all day and that was a one-stop shop.

"I love it, so far so good," she said as we were then greeted by the owners.

"Hello, I'm Mrs. Lons, but you can call me Karen. My husband and I were expecting a potential homebuyer today. I take it you two are a part of the tour. Are your parents going to join us shortly?" she questioned nicely.

Channy and I had that, black don't crack smile on our faces. It felt good to represent a young black power couple that were about to purchase our first home together.

"I'm her zaddy, and this is my babe," I said proudly. I put my arm around her with my chest out. Channy gave me a quick elbow in my side as she laughed.

"Don't mind him, he has a dry sense of humor. I'm who you spoke with yesterday. We're the potential home buyers, but I just want you to know, how excited I am right now!" Channy expressed her joy.

I didn't know what it is about a woman, no matter what color they were. They could always get excited for each other, when their man was about to do something special for them.

Mrs. Karen read Channy's happy facial expressions showed how she had me in check. She took her by the hand and left me standing in the same spot.

"What just happened?" I questioned. When I looked up, I saw a man come from out the garage, headed my way.

"There he is, I'm Mr. Lons, but you can call me Kevin. Putt'er there, pal," Mr. Lons said as he extended his hand.

"How are you doing, Mr. Lons, I'm Chance," I said and greeted him with a firm handshake.

Men aren't like women. To me, when a man seemed to be a little overly excited or smiled too hard when I first met them, made me feel uncomfortable. As if I couldn't trust them, but that was just me used to being around thugs. I never paid attention to the fact, that everybody didn't grow up like I did.

"Well, Chance, it's nice to meet you. And judging by the strength of your handshake, you're a very stern individual," he said.

He must've felt that I was uneased, and that was a good icebreaker. His proper introduction helped me to understand that not everyone was out to hurt or get over on me. I then let my guard down.

"Okay, thanks for noticing. This house looks like it was well-invested in," I mentioned. Although, I could only see the front of the house, it did look nice.

I really wished we could've waited until I got drafted into the NFL first. I could've purchased her a mansion, but being that she was carrying my seed, I'd already proposed, and I wasn't sure how my surgery would've turned out, I felt like that was the move for the moment.

"Yeah, the Mrs. made sure of it, and now, she's

ready to buy another one and do it all over again," he said as he looked off into to space like I did, when I told Choyce I was going to buy Channy a house.

Men said yes to anything under the pressure of their woman's request.

"Hey, Chance, let's go in the garage and drink a few beers," he said to snap me back into reality.

He must've felt what I was going through. After I found out what I had gotten myself into, it made me wanna have a drink or two.

"Great minds think alike. Say no more and lead the way." Mr. Lons talked my language.

I didn't feel like I was the only one that got punked by someone, who was only five foot even, if not shorter. After a few Heineken's, I was in good spirit and ready to get down to business.

"Tell me a little history about this house, Mr. Lons?" I asked since the garage was the only part, I was going to see for myself.

"Chance, this is a six-bedroom, five full and one-half bathroom, four car garage with a in ground pool out back. And the Mrs. wants six-hundred thousand."

"Wow, I didn't expect to hear such a steep price. I was thinking a little lower," I said. I had the money, and it was a very nice home for that price, but I had to see if I could talk him down.

"I'm mean, hell, Chance. We put a lot of money into this house. With all the upgrades that we did, I can't go too much lower," he explained.

I noticed when he said the word lower. He looked out of the corner of his eye, thinking that his wife was about to walk right in.

After a couple of more beers, we ended up settling for $398,500 cash. We even shook on it. I thought I was being slick.

"Kevin!" Mrs. Lons yelled as she stormed into the garage

"Let them have it for three hundred thousand flat!" she said with the biggest smile on her face.

"No, Karen. It's going for $398 and some change. Chance and I already shook on it. Isn't that right, partner?"

"Yeah, um, wow. Yes, we did," I answered, and then learned that when money was involved, anybody could've been a hustler, even an old white man.

"Okay, if that's what the man said, then that's what it will be," Karen said and made a face at Channy.

"I told you, we can spend money better than them," she said, and they laughed together.

"Well, babe, you should've just stayed in the car," Channy joked, and they laughed some more. I decided to leave the negotiating up to her, from that point on.

"I guess you're right, babe," I said, then looked down at all my empty beer bottles. Never again.

"Don't worry, Chance, Kevin has come a long way. And today was the first time that he made a good deal over me. Isn't that right, honey?"

"Yes, dear," he replied, then held his half-empty beer bottle in the air and took his last swig.

"Yes, well, Mr. Coleman here has a long time to figure it out, too. Let's say a lifetime's worth of it." Channy smiled as she leaned forward and gave me a kiss.

"Aww, that's the type of love that me and him used to be in," Mrs. Lons said with a sweet grin on her face.

"Used to be?" Mr. Lons said. He had a confused look on his face as everyone laughed but him.

We shook hands then gave them time to get their paperwork together, so we could get them paid and get a move-in date.

"Well, Chance, I tried to save you some money, but you had to be the man of this situation," Channy joked.

"Yeah, and I see from now on, I need to stay in my own lane," I assured as I drove off, and felt as if I had made the right move for me and my family.

*****

"How do you feel, babe" We did it--our first home," I questioned and looked at her.

We were in my car, and I had my seat back. It was a blessing to see that smile on her face. While I looked at her, I could picture her in a wedding dress. She was about to be Mrs. Coleman.

"I feel wonderful, babe. I'm blessed to have you in my life. I knew ever since the night of our prom, that I wanted to spend the rest of my life with you," she said, with that dreamy glare in her eyes that made my heart melt.

"I have been in love with you since middle school. I just didn't know how to approach you, because how close we were as friends. And the feeling that you had at prom; I felt the same way from day one."

I fell in love with the fact that she'd been fine her entire life, but she saved herself for me and me only. She had the kinda love that if I made it to the NFL or not, she was my sworn ride or die.

"Thank you for taking your time with me. It made me appreciate you more, and now I'm about to give birth to our first child. I believe this baby is going to be special because he was conceived while we were still pure and innocent," Channy said as she looked at her stomach while she rubbed on it.

"I love you, babe, and I'm proud of us."

"I love you too, babe."

Chapter 7

Choyce called me over, so I could see what he had done to the house. He also had something to run past me.

"I see you moved into the entire upstairs," I joked as I looked around.

He had it remolded and decked the fuck out. He had all the walls removed from mom's to his room. It looked like a bedroom in a mansion, and he had a jacuzzi, full bath, walk-in closet, and a walk-in shower. He had bulky furniture with a California King bed, flat screens, surround sound, and of course, a stripper pole.

"Off top, wait until you see what I'm about to have done to the downstairs, lil' bruh. You're a smart man, owning our own construction company was the move. This damn near didn't cost shit," he said with a proud grin.

"Thank you, so what's on your mind, big bro?" I questioned as flopped down on the couch.

"I was checking on the progress of one the house

out south when I ran across a dude that we to high school wit, named Reco," Choyce said as he dropped his head in disbelief.

"He'd always been a loudmouth, fast-talking nigga. I sold him a couple ounces back then. But when I saw him recently, he told me it was a lot of money out south."

"He told me how many kilos and pounds he moved out there. I fronted him two keys, and he came back with one-hundred bands in three days."

"I threw five more his way, and here it is, a little over two weeks, and I'm still waiting. Word around town is he's out here riding good like he don't owe," Choyce finished.

"What's the move, bro?" I questioned.

"At first, he wouldn't answer my calls, so I called from my other phone. Once he answered, he told had my money and to pick it up tonight. I don't trust that nigga, lil' bruh, he sent me his location, and I just need for you to ride with me."

"Say less, it's a play then," I agreed.

3:30 a.m.

We arrived at the address and parked three houses down.

"Look, Chance, we're going in here to play it coo, wit this nigga. I'm coming to pick up a lot of money. If he tries anything, we gotta kill that nigga," Choyce said as he reached in his backseat to grab his empty duffle bag.

"Nah, for real. But don't do this shit anymore, bro. Fuck the front game, since when did you start doing that shit? If he pays with no problem, tonight, then cut that nigga off for good. Where's our guns?" I questioned.

"Damn, lil' bruh, this shit got me all fucked-up. Pop the trunk right quick," Choyce said as we got out.

We secured our guns in the smalls of our backs underneath our shirts. We looked each other over, to made sure they weren't noticeable, then headed to across the street to the house.

"Who is?" Reco asked.

"It's me, Choyce."

Reco opened the door with coke all in his nostrils and acted slow as fuck.

"Damn, nigga, I forget you was a twin. I thought, I was seeing double," he joked and let us in.

"This my lil' bruh, Chance," Choyce introduced as we shook up. Choyce set his duffle bag down, and we took a seat.

Reco took a seat in front of a table that had ten rolled blunts laid on some coke dust.

"Now, what's with the empty bag?" he questioned.

"I bought it to collect my money. I hope you didn't think, we were going to leave out of here, with almost one-hundred and fifty bands in our hands, did you?" Choyce questioned.

Choyce then looked over at me, and I could already tell it was going to be some bullshit involved.

"Pick up your money?" Reco questioned, then got out his straw and snorted another line.

"Oh, that's what you're here for. I forgot, I talked

to you earlier," he said as he took a shot of liquor then lit up a blunt.

"You came to collect, just in time. I just got this hoe ass nigga out of ah hundred bands, and eighty bricks two days ago! I can't even move this shit fast enough," he said.

He tilted his head back and stuck his finger in his shot glass. He then dripped liquor down each one of his nostrils. I'd never seen no shit like it; I just thought that was his way of getting high and to each there own.

"You got eighty bricks here, right now? Nigga, you bullshittin?" Choyce asked then looked at me out of the corner of his eye.

"I kid you not. I got three things that I don't lie about, nigga. That's my dick, money, and drugs. It's all downstairs right now," Reco boasted as he took a puff from his blunt.

He tried to pass it to me, but I saw it had on some coke before he lit it. So, I didn't want no parts.

"Damn, I should've asked y'all to bring some Swishers," Reco said. As he leaned his head back to catch his drain, I could see that his powder high had left him.

Reco reached on side of his chair and grabbed a kilo. He sat it on the table, but it had Blacks stamp on it.

"Here's one of the bricks right here," he said as he pulled out a knife and cut it open. He put the tip of it to his nose full of cocaine then snorted.

"If y'all wanna see the rest of them, come downstairs," Reco offered.

I could tell Choyce was heated as we watched Reco roll up a hundred-dollar bill and snorted his line out of one of the kilos he got from bro.

"Aye, where was them niggas from, on that lick you hit?" Choyce questioned as he sat up on the edge of the couch.

"Fort Lauderdale, Florida," Reco answered. Choyce just shook his head.

"Fuck it, let me see them bricks. Maybe we can work out a deal for the money you owe me," Choyce suggested.

We walked down to the basement. Reco wasn't lying; he had bricks stacked up ten high on two picnic tables. As I looked around, he had money stacked from the top, to the bottom of a four by three gun safe and stupid pounds of weed on each side of it.

"Like I said, I've been robbing niggas, for about four months straight," Reco said as he leaned down to pick up a kilo.

"So, don't think I don't know a setup, when I see one." Reco stood back up and had two Desert Eagles, pointed at me and Choyce.

"Aye, we just came to collect what you owed, my brother. We're not here to rob shit," I explained with my hands up.

"Shut the fuck up! You niggas come in my house, with empty bags and shit! Talking about I owe you. Nigga, I'm Reco! I don't owe nobody shit!" he said.

When I looked him in his eyes, they were blood shot red. The look on his face was so frowned up, he looked like a demon.

"Man, fuck it, you owe me not him. Let my little brother go, this is between me and you," Choyce suggested.

"Nigga, you must think I'm stupid. Why the fuck would I let him leave a murder scene?" Reco said. The more he'd talked, the eviler he'd become.

"I want both you niggas to strip!" he demanded as he fired shots from both guns over our heads.

"Alright! Hold up!" Choyce said. He started with his shirt; he took it off slowly. I saw all his attention was on Choyce.

So, I acted as if I was taking mine off too because he hadn't looked my way. My gun was tucked in my lower back. I had time to grab it, once I had my hand on it.

"Nigga, don't think I forgot about you!" he said as he pointed both his guns at me.

That's when Choyce shot'em like three times.

"Fuck you!" he yelled. He was so high off coke, that the bullets didn't faze him. He turned as if he wanted to shoot Choyce.

Before he could pull the trigger, I shot him twice. He had been hit at least five times. He dropped down to one knee, with his guns pointed at the both of us.

He got a few shot off in my direction. I took cover, and Choyce shot him again in the neck and mouth. That was what killed him.

"Here, bro, take this bag. It's time for us to go to work," Choyce said as he tossed me a duffle bag.

He ran upstairs and came down with three more bags.

"I saw these in the kitchen. Hurry up, lil' bruh, grab what you can," Choyce ordered.

We came up from the basement with two of the bags filled with money. We filled the one we had with a as many keys we could fit in there and the other one with pounds.

"You didn't touch shit, did you, lil' bruh?" Choyce questioned, after we made our second trip.

We had left too many drugs behind. We dumped all the money in the trunk of our car, then went back and got as much as we could.

"Hell nah, but slow this car down, bro. You know we're on the hot ass southside, it's way too federal in this car right now to be smashing."

"My bad, lil' bruh. I got you, I just got some fucked-up images in my head right now. I had to shoot that fuck nigga in the mouth because he talked too much."

"It's coo, bro. What's done is done. He had it coming. He was out here playing ah dirty game; it was either us or him. He just got fucked all the way around."

*****

Once we pulled up to our warehouse, I had to let bro know how I felt.

"I'm telling you, bro! We keep on wildin out and making our own rules to life, we going to end up dead or in prison!" I said as I got out the car and ran up in his face.

"What do you mean, lil' bruh? Niggas was out here trying to take advantage of us, trying to extort you! We out here, fuck these bitch ass niggas!" Choyce said as he tried his best to defend his actions.

"We haven't done shit! That didn't need to be done, that's all I know!" he yelled. We were then face to face with our fist balled up, ready to fight at any moment.

"The whole city is talking about us by name. This shit is crazy, we gotta get our shit together, bro!" I had to speak my mind out of concern for us.

"What else do you have to prove out here? We're way too smart to be living like this!" I said. Choyce just gave me a cold stare down.

"Man, get the fuck out my face. Because I'm about to knock you the fuck out," Choyce replied.

I didn't know what came over me, but I tackled him down to the ground. I hit him a couple times in his jaw. He, somehow, came from under and overpowered me. He then had his forearm pressed against my throat.

"I told you to get the fuck out my face! You damn right, I'm out here striking fear in people's hearts! I'm out here makin money and gettin hated on by these fuck ass niggas!" He yelled as he applied more pressure.

"You'd better be lucky you're my little brother, or I'd beat the shit out of you," Choyce said with a crazy ass Charles Manson look in his eyes.

"Man, I love you," he said as let me up.

"Fuck this shit! You need a team, bro! That nigga

was crazy as fuck, and he could've killed both of us!" I yelled.

My life had flashed before my eyes too many times; I was tired of it. I didn't know when the madness was going to end. A part of it wasn't our fault, and a part of it was. If we never lived that life, we wouldn't have had to defend ourselves so much.

"I know, lil' bruh! But these niggas ain't sloid, and you know that shit!" Choyce said as he paced back and forth.

"Niggas is on that fuck shit, and you're the only person I can trust!" Choyce yelled in frustration.

"Get the fuck out the game then! Why are you so ready to play with your life, every fucking day, bro?" I questioned. I'd had enough of that shit.

I just wanted to walk away and never speak another word to him.

"I can't, bro! I got so much blood on my hands, that I'm tied in for life. As soon as I try to find a way out, I'm going to get killed. You can leave if you want to! But

I ain't going no fuckin where," Choyce said as he turned his back to me.

That was my opportunity; I could've said fuck everything and walked away. I had a feeling if I did, that was the last time I would've ever seen my brother alive.

If I would've told him no on that last mission, it could've been the last time. I just couldn't leave him out there like that.

"Come on, bro, let's get this shit put up. I love you too," I said.

Chapter 8

All Good Things Don't Last

It was the first night in the new house, and Channy and I loved it, but when it was time to lay down, I couldn't sleep. I hadn't talked to Choyce in going on a month, but I could feel something was wrong. It was 4:30 a.m., and he hit my line.

"What's good, bro?" I answered as I tried not to wake her up.

"I need for you to ride with me right quick, you ready?" I could tell something wasn't right by the pause between his words.

"Yeah, pull up, bro."

I was dressed and in the living room by the time bro pulled up. When I saw his headlights pull in the driveway, I locked up the house and got in his car.

"What's up, Choyce? What's on your mind?" I questioned.

He had a still look on his face, like he wanted to vent but didn't know where to start. He had a smoke sack and Swisher on the dash. So, I rolled up before he pulled off.

"Lil' bruh, this may sound crazy, but I'm ready to get out the game," Choyce said, and I somehow knew that's what he wanted to tell me.

That was a very tough decision for him to have made, and I could see that he had been battling with himself. Once again, I was glad I could be there for him.

"What made you have a change of heart?" I questioned.

"After we got into it and hadn't talked for a few weeks, I had time to look in the mirror and think over my life. I saw it was so much more I could be doing besides this shit," Choyce went on to say.

"It's hard though, lil' bruh. I'm trying everything I can think of, but I just can't find a passion for shit but these streets. It's like I'm running from her, but she keeps calling my name," he explained as I passed the blunt to him.

"The game made me who I am. My only regret is the day I pulled you in on our first lick. I wish, I never introduced you to this shit, but at the end of the day, you handled your business. Now, if your surgery doesn't go right, you already got NFL money."

"I love you, Chance. I would be dead or in prison, right now, if it weren't for you. I owe you my life," Choyce said.

"I love you too, bro, and you already know. Every move you'd ever made, I've always been right by your side ever since we were kids."

"We just bumped heads with each other and have to let our names cool down from the streets. Everything happens for a reason," I said as I passed the blunt back to him.

He had dark bags under his eyes like he hadn't slept in weeks. He was tired, and I could tell that might've been a cry for help. If I would've told him I was chilling, and to call me later, there was no telling what he would've done to get his stress out.

"We needed a little time apart, but I already told you, I got your back. I can't go back on my word. I just need you to respect the fact that I got a family now, and

I'm still looking forward to my future," I explained.

"Nah, for real, I understand. We're older now, so it's time to choose a path and stick with it. Here's the thing, I'm expecting something from Black, in a couple of days. It's nothing too big but enough to exit the game. I'm ah make that my last run then I'm done. Are you down to fuck wit me one last time?" Choyce questioned.

"Say less, I got you. On some other shit, I know we got our other business up and running, but what are we going to do about our night club?"

"Keep it a twenty-one and over club. I've been letting Muhammed run it, and he's been doing his thing. That's how he's been able to catch up with the mortgage on his car garage. We'll just let him partner with us and let that shit work itself out.

*****

Bro called me two days later and told me to pull up to the library asap.

When I walked in, he had a confused look on his face. There were so many crates, I got so nervous and wanted to turn around and leave.

145

"What the fuck is this, bro?" I questioned as I counted how many crates there were.

"Lil' bruh, how in the fuck did Black get thirty-two crates delivered? I'm starting to think that nigga's the feds, straight up," Choyce said.

"Nah, for real. I wouldn't had accepted all this shit, if I were you," I said as I looked out the window. I didn't see any feds, but that didn't mean they weren't around.

"You think, I would've? I told you the other day, I was expecting something like the first time. When the delivery came, I signed off on it, and they just started bringing them in like this."

"I closed the door after the first twelve, wondering why they took them so far back. They knocked on the door again, talking about I had had more. So, I wanted to wait until you got here before I called to see if this was some sort of mistake.

Choyce made the call, and I kept looking out the window.

"Black, right on for the packages, but I didn't

order—" Choyce said, then stopped talking for a second.

"Okay. What's up, Lil Black? Let me holler at your brother right quick."

"Okay, well, when he gets back, let him know," Choyce said and paused again.

"Man, what? Don't tell me that shit, bro, that can't be true. We were just down there." Choyce then took a seat on one of the crates and hung his head low.

"Bro, man fuck! Over some dumb shit like that? Ok, I got you bro, I'll keep it solid with you. I'll take care of it, and sorry about your loss. Just know you still got two brothers over here. And we're going to keep this shit going. Off top." Choyce ended the call and continued to shake his head in belief.

"Damn, bro. Is it all bad?" I asked. I was fucked-up about what I'd thought, I heard.

"Black got caught up in a cartel war, and he didn't make it. Shit's all fucked-up," Choyce said and was truly hurt behind that news.

Black was the only dude that Choyce had love for outside of me. And he was then just a memory like

Justin.

"Lil Black said they been on a killing spree. Killing up both sides of the Colombians and Mexicans cartels. He gave us these crates to split," Choyce explained as we looked at them.

"He's asking in return, if we can get twelve off for him and send the currency back to help him rebuild his garrison. The war took place on his turf, and they tore it up. I told him that it's ah go, but I'm all fucked-up behind this one."

"Damn, bro. I kinda felt that was going to happen when he told me he did business with both sides of the cartels," I said as I stopped looking out the window and took a seat.

"I know, I just hate that he went out like that, but we're going to get this shit gone and send that money."

"Nah, for real. I'm with the shit, bro, we can have this shit in rotation in no time. They showed us a lot of love there, and they didn't have to. So, let's send it back to them," I agreed.

I was mad hurt about what happened to Black.

He died like a true king though, so helping him rebuild his kingdom, was a way to send my condolences.

"This is how we're going to start this off. We're going to open the club in a week. That will give enough us time to promote. Then we can make our move on the city.

"We haven't been out here in the streets in a month. So, we should be able to hit the game hard and keep a low profile," Choyce explained.

"That's good for us. By the time they catch wind of our movement, it will be too late. This time, less blood and more money. We can't put everybody on, bro. If we keep trustin these niggah, then this shit isn't ever going to work," I clarified before I agreed to play any part in that shit.

"So, from now on, we have to pick wisely. Fuck school buddies and all other non-go gettas. It's wrap for that those types," I continued.

"Nah, for real. They weren't even worthy enough, to eat the scraps from the table anyway, lil' bruh," Choyce agreed.

"Off top, but even if we only deal with niggas from out of town to get this shit off. That's what the fuck we're going to do because the cemetery will be full of them weak-minded individuals from our city if we don't avoid trusting our shit in their hands. Some people just aren't cut out for this shit, fuck'em though, it's time for us to eat," I demanded.

*****

It was two weeks later, and the city acted like they were starving. In that short period, we'd been gone, we'd gotten those twelve keys off for Lil Black and sent him the money asap.

That must've opened a window for u, because when we did right by him, money started flowing our way. We didn't have to kill nobody, and everybody had they money right when they shopped with us.

"Good morning, babe," Channy said as she rushed to brushed her teeth then got dressed.

Her boutique had taken off, she'd been busy, busy. Her clothes had been on the front cover of magazines. She had country singers, rap artist, R&B stars,

150

and fashion models rocking her brand. She was making money, and that had her beyond excited about her dream.

"Good morning, babe, don't forget to drop those clothes off for that photoshoot," I said as a reminder. Her schedule had been crazy, even though she had a planner, I sometimes had to help her out.

"Oh shit, I forgot all about that. Thank you for reminding me. It was just a summer dress I'm supposed to send through UPS today. If you have time could you drop it off for me?" she asked as she walked out the bathroom butt naked into her walk-in closet.

Her ass was so round, and it jiggled with each step she took. That baby weight had her juicier than what she already was. I got out the bed and walked in the closet behind her.

"Damn, bae. Your ass is looking heavy today, let me tune you up right quick before we get our day started," I said as I kissed the side of her neck.

"Okay, zaddy. But you gotta be quick and don't go in so deep," she said as she held onto the back of her vanity chair. I licked my fingers and got her walls wet, then slid it in for the early morning quickie.

"Who's is this?" I questioned as I smacked her hard on the ass.

"It's all yours, zaddy! Oh yes, smack my ass again like that," she said. After I laid the pound game down, I was ready to take a shower.

"Babe, be careful out there, today. I've been having bad vibes ever since I woke up," Channy warned as she came into the bathroom.

I had just wiped the steam off the mirror with my towel. When I looked at my reflection, I remembered the last time she said that, was the day I had gotten shot.

"Off top, babe. Like I said, I'm just going to keep this going until I get my surgery next month, then I'm out. Thanks for the warning, and I love you," I assured as I wrapped my towel around my waist then grabbed my toothbrush.

"Well, I love you too, and you know I got your back. I'm still upset it took you so long to tell me. I could've been put you up on game." She smiled as she walked out the bathroom.

"What you know about the streets?" I questioned as I peeked my head out the bathroom.

"You know I got a brother doing eighty-five years right now. You don't get that kinda time, for doing small shit."

"Oh, and by the way, stop by the car garage today. When I went to pick up my G-Wagon, I talked with Muhammed. I got you something for supporting me, the way you have. I just made the final payment this morning. Plus, since my baby zaddy is a boss ass nigga, I felt it's time he rode like one," Channy said as she grabbed her purse and bags.

"Thank you, babe," I said. She had me geeked up to get my day started.

As I watched her walk out the room, I was amazed with the woman she had become. I was able to watch the woman of my dreams grow right in front of my eyes ever since middle school.

I got dressed and had to apply my drip for the day. Since she got me something new to ride, I had to flex in it.

I called Choyce to see where he was at, so we could link up.

"I'm at the club, lil' bruh, come through, and niggah, wait until you see what your queen got you. I got Muhammed ordering my one, right now!" Choyce rejoiced.

"Off top, bro. She just told me before she left the house. I'm on my way," I said, then ended the call.

After I got dressed, I had to pause for a second. I was impressed to see the work our construction company had done to our upstairs.

I had to follow suit with bro and had the entire upstairs turned into a master bedroom. We had his and hers walk-in closets, his and hers sinks in the bathrooms, walk-in shower, and all. I had our baby's nursery set up not too far from our bed, but I had to wait on the color for the gender reveal.

Channy had a massive kitchen built and what I called a getaway house, but she called it a *she shed* in the backyard. It looked just like a one-bedroom apartment on the inside. I had the entire basement to myself, and I turned it into a part fitness room, part mancave.

Babe bought me a Ferragamo fit. I still wasn't into fashion like that, but she was a fashion designer. So, I was like her protege because she wanted to eventually start making men's clothes.

After I got dressed, then grabbed the package babe asked me to deliver, I headed up to car garage.

*****

"Lil' bruh, check this out. Nobody in the city, is up on this yet," Choyce said as I walked in and stopped in my tracks.

Babe got me an all-red and chromed out 2020 Jaguar F-type. It had chrome and red Forgiato rims with the five-point star design. The inside was peanut butter brown, soft leather with red trim and stitching. It didn't have tints, so I was riding fishbowl.

"How much did she pay for this, Muhammed?" I questioned.

I loved the car, but if she paid what I'd thought she did, I was going to put that right back into her bank account. She worked too hard to get to where she was. I didn't want her to blow her profit on me.

"She dropped fifty bands on it. But it costed one-hundred and some change. I had to get this one though because how excited she was. I knew if I got it, you would make good on the other fifty, plus all the extras," Muhammed explained.

"Don't worry, lil' bruh. I already looked out, we workin out of the same banking system anyway. So, it's all paid for. But wait until you hear this," Choyce said as he pulled out his phone and pressed play to Young Dolph featuring Megan thee Stallion's *R&B.*

"Off top! Muhammed, you got this bitch knocking!" I said as I jumped in.

On top of how the car looked, it had massive bass game.

"I'll get up with y'all later, I gotta go drop something off for babe right quick," I said as I connected to my Bluetooth. I had to run that song back as I flexed on the city.

I put on the Ferragamo shades, bae got me to go with my fit and backed out. I felt like a true boss. I pulled up to the UPS and left my car running as I grabbed the package off the passenger seat and ran in right quick.

"Damn, you smell good! What you got on?" some female asked when I walked in.

"I don't know. Something my wife got me, but I gotta drop this off for a next-day delivery," I said as I dropped the package on the desk.

"Do you already have an account? If not, give me your number, I got a UPS you could drop off overnight deliveries in, if you'd like," she questioned.

I didn't even look her over; Channy was a dime, and she was a penny. There was no comparison, so I just brushed her little invite off.

"Nah, it's already one in my wife's name," I said then gave Channy's number to her.

"Girl, who you out here flirting with now?" some other girl came from the back said, then quickly turned around.

I saw her, and she looked very familiar, but she'd turned around too quick.

"This, Ferragamo god right here," the girl

answered, but when she turned around, the other one had already gone to the back.

"Well, damn, more for me then. The total is $10.21, sir," she said and waited on me to pull out money, but I paid with card instead.

Once I got the tracking number, I left the store, took a picture, then sent it to Channy.

As I pulled off, I saw both the girls in the window. I then noticed it was the girl from Channy's barbeque. The one I suspected set up the play when Channy got shot. She was on her phone once again.

Channy then facetimed me.

"Babe, how do you like my gift?" she questioned with a proud grin from ear to ear.

"I love it. Thank you, babe. You got me out here bossed-up," I said, then I pulled into the next parking lot and parked.

"Yeah, I figured you'd like and it. I got it in your favorite color," she said.

When I looked her in the eyes, she just looked happy, and she was in her element. I hired our construction company to remodel her boutique. It looked very professional. She had so many clients, and she was able to hire help. She was a real boss.

"What you are doing, babe?" she questioned.

"Nothing, just admiring your beauty," I answered. Even though I was using my other phone to look up a catering service. Her favorite food was seafood, so I hired a personal chef.

I ordered king crab legs, lobster tails, Comeaux's smoked alligator sausage, Louisiana crawfish, and everything else that came in a seafood boil. All I had to do was pick up the liquor.

"Well, I gotta huge order to fill, I'll just see you when I get home," Channy said.

"Okay, what time are you coming?" I questioned.

"I should be there about 10:30 p.m."

*****

It was 9:45 when I walked into the kitchen, and the catering company that I hired, had babe's kitchen twerking. They'd even set us up a nice candlelit dinner table. I had the wine chilled on ice. I knew she'd probably

159

drink half a glass because of the pregnancy. So, I had my fifth of D'usse in the freezer.

I had a missed call, and someone needed a key. Babe had told me she was running late. So, I texted to let her know. She wanted me to stay, but I went anyway. By the time I made it back, I had time to get in the shower and get ready for her to walk through the door.

"Hey, babe. It smells good as fuck in here. Where are you?" Channy said as she walked in.

"I'm in the dining room, babe," I answered. I didn't greet her at the door because I wanted to see her face when she walked around the corner.

"What's that I smell, babe?" she questioned again. When she walked around the corner, she paused and covered her mouth.

"Are those for me?" she asked with a surprised look on her face.

"Yes, babe. You went out your way to make me feel special, so this is my way of saying you thank you," I said, then handed her a bouquet of roses.

When she smelled them, I stepped to the side to

show her the candlelight on top of our decorated dinner table.

"Chance, babe, thank you so much," she said and started to cry. Ever since she'd been pregnant, she'd been very emotional.

"Don't cry, babe, follow me." I took her by the hand and led her upstairs.

I had rose peddles that led from the top stair to the bed and stopped before the bathroom. I had Bath and Body Works scented candles lit everywhere.

"You don't have any idea about the day I just had. I really appreciate this," she said, then laid her head on my chest.

"Don't worry, babe, days like this come wit it. I'm just thankful that I was here to comfort you," I said, and I kissed her forehead.

"Take you ah shower, babe, I'm about to go set up the table. It's seafood, your favorite." I heard Channy cry from the time I left the room until I got to the bottom of the stairs.

After I got the table ready, I got my fifth of

D'usse out the freezer and a shot glass. I poured my shot. I tilted my head back to drink but felt the cold steel from the barrel of a gun.

"Don't move, nigga, take us to your stash right mufuckin now!" whoever it was, demanded.

"Listen, all my money is in the basement. I'll take you to it, right now. Just be coo, it will be worth it," I pleaded.

I didn't have any money in the house, but I knew Channy was upstairs. I just wanted to get dude as far away from her as possible.

"You two take him downstairs, I'll check the rest of the house. I see an apartment out back. This stupid mufuckah probably got something stashed out there," I heard someone order.

I felt my heart drop to the bottom of my feet. It was three of them, and I felt defenseless.

"Nah, there's nothing else in the house or out there, it's all downstairs," I said and hoped I'd convinced them to follow me.

"Fuck you, nigga! Shut the fuck up!" I heard

someone yell as I got knocked in the back of my head with the butt of his gun.

I dropped to one knee; it was hard enough to feel, but not hard enough to knock me out.

"Okay, let's get this over with. The basement is this way," I said.

I stood to my feet and led the way. I turned my head and saw the third dude start in the living room first.

"Turn around and take us to the money! If you make any more sudden moves, I'm ah blast you, bitch ass nigga!" the guy with the gun, demanded.

We got to the downstairs, and I turned on the light. I'd taken my reputation for granted. All the weapons I had in the house, were in the upstairs bedroom. I did have an empty gun safe down there though. I walked them over to it and pretended like it was filled with money.

"It's all in here, you can have it," I said as I knelt to do the combination.

"Hurry up, nigga, I ain't got all day! Yo! Get that bag ready," I heard him say.

I knew when he asked that question, he had taken his eyes off me, for that split second. I knew the other dude would've averted his attention, to get the bag ready. It was then or never.

I moved my head back and turned it towards the stairs. I then used my left hand to grab his wrist. It all happened in a matter of seconds.

"Get this nigga!" I heard the dude yell out as he hit me twice in my eye and jaw, with his free hand. I had already stood to my feet and used my righthand to cuff him by the hamstring.

"Get out the way!" I heard the other one yell out.

I heard five shots from dude I had on my back and four more from the dude behind us.

I felt the one on my back go limp. He laid awkwardly on my back and was too heavy to hold, so I had to drop him.

"Don't move, nigga! Stay right there!" dude said. He'd just shot and killed his partner and had the gun pointed at me.

I couldn't see who he was because he had a mask

on. I heard the door to the basement open.

"The fuck just happened, did he make a move or something?" I heard the other dude yell out, followed by a single shot. Dude did a half-flip, then rolled down the steps and landed at the bottom awkwardly.

"Babe!" Channy yelled out, but I had a gun pointed at me and couldn't respond.

"Come on, man, the fuck is you waiting on?" I questioned because he still hadn't shot me.

He just kept franticly, looking over at the gun closest to him then back at me. That's when I looked at his hand, his gun wasn't cocked. He had run out of bullets.

I reached for the gun by my feet. At that same time, he went for the one by the basement steps.

"Stop, nigga! Don't do it! Tell me what I want to know, and you can walk out of here right fuckin now!" I demanded. He hesitated for a second, then went for it anyway.

"You're just going have to kill me," dude said as he made it over to the gun, right before he secured it in his hand. I pulled the trigger, but the gun jammed.

"I not going anywhere until you empty that safe," dude demanded. He took a side-step towards the bag then kicked it over to me.

"Okay. You got it, bro. Just don't shoot me," I said, then dropped the gun and put both my hands in the air.

When I turned my back towards him, I heard two more shots.

"Ahh shit! I heard him yell out. I turned around he had been shot twice in the shoulder.

He dropped to one knee, and his gun fell on the floor. Before he could pick it back up, I ran over to him. I stomped kicked him in his chest so hard, his head dented the drywall.

"Who set sent you to my house, nigga!" I questioned, then snatched off his ski mask.

"Come on, man. I didn't even wanna do this shit!" he yelled.

"Who sent you, nigga! I don't wanna hear about shit else." Right then, his cell phone rang. I hurried to get it out his pocket.

"Who's this!" I questioned.

"What the fuck is taking you niggas so long? I'm about to pull the fuck off!" I heard someone yell on the other end.

"If you don't wanna end up dead, like the rest of these niggas, then that's what the fuck you better do." I ended the call, but his phone locked instantly.

"What's the code, nigga!" I demanded.

"2444!" he hurried to say. I looked through his messages. I saw one from earlier in the day.

Cuzz, I know where that nigga that killed Noah live.

That's when I thought back; it was that same bitch from UPS. If I would've known that bitch, was the one who went back into the room, I would've never shipped Channy's package from there. Once I'd left, and I saw her in the window, I should've gone back in there and put the fear of God in her heart. None of that shit would've happened.

"Chance!" Channy yelled as she came downstairs.

"Babe, I'm sorry," I said as I grabbed ahold of her.

"How the fuck did they know where you lived! I told you not to go make that last play! They must've followed you home! You out there moving too sloppy!" she screamed.

"Babe, chill. They didn't follow me, and it had nothing to do with my play. Look," I said as I passed her dude's phone.

"I never told you, but the day you got shot, I killed that nigga for you. This text was sent from that same bitch, you went off on the day of your party. She works at the UPS, I dropped your package off at," I explained.

"Okay, well me and mine are going to pay that bitch a visit tomorrow," she said.

The entire time I talked to Channy, I had taken my eyes off dude that was still alive.

I right when I put my arms back around her, I heard a gunshot.

I paused for a second as I expected to fall dead any second. When I noticed I was ok, I checked Channy out, and she was fine. When I looked her in the eyes, they were filled with tears.

"It's okay, babe, it was either us or them," I assured her as I took the gun from her hand.

When I turned around, dude had made it back to his guy's gun. He had it pointed right at me. Channy had saved my life, once again.

"Go get dressed and call the police, babe. Tell them it's been a murder."

Final Chapter

My going away party

It was the end of the summer, and my surgery was scheduled for the following week. My doctor explained that I had healed tremendously, but the surgery was still only a fifty-fifty chance that I'd be able to perform on the field like I used to. He also assured me, not everyone's surgery turned out the same. Some healed way better than others.

"Well, babe, you're one step closer to making your dream come true. How does that make you feel?" Channy questioned. She laid on her mom's couch and rubbed her stomach as I gave her a foot massage.

She'd been staying at her mom's because she was under a lot of stress. I'd been there with her the entire time. After what took place in our home, we hurried to get it remolded, then put it up for sale asap.

"I mean, my coach agreed that I can rehab from the University of Alabama to get me ready for the upcoming football season. There's a strong possibility,

I'll be able to play," I answered.

"It's okay, babe, you will, just have faith. I did my research on those type of surgeries, and you'll be alright. You just gotta protect yourself, that's all," she assured.

"Nah, for real. I'm just glad you're attending with me. God really has made a way for us to be together, after all we've been through," I said as I moved her feet off the couch, then placed them on my lap.

I talked Channy into checking into her scholarship. Her boutique had taken off, but she had a bigger vision for herself. Graduating from college was a part of her goals. Once she sent them an email to explain her story, they accepted it and allowed her to attend as well. We decided to relocate there, and we found a home close to campus.

"Are you sure, you don't wanna go to my party with me, tonight?" I questioned as I looked over at her.

"Hell nah, I'm good. You and your brother stress me the fuck out," Channy laughed.

"But, for real, I gotta make a few calls. Plus, I'm

training someone to help my mom run my boutique for me while I'm gone. I'll be back and forth as much as I can, but I gotta make sure they know what to do," she answered.

"It's coo, I'm not going to stay that long anyway. I'm about to go handle a few things. I love you, and I'll see you later," I said.

"I love you too, and be careful, babe."

******

Choyce had thrown us a going away party for him leaving the game and me going off to school.

"I can't lie, bro. This is bittersweet because I finally get to pursue my dream. Once I leave here, my life will head in a whole new direction. I won't be able to have your back from so far away," I stressed my concern.

As we sat in our office, I stared at the newspaper headlined *College bad boy, Chance Coleman, maybe returning to the football field after murder allegations*. A letter from my coach sat on the desktop right in front of me.

"I can't lie, lil' bruh, you wouldn't give up. You

just don't know how much you inspired me. Don't worry about leaving, though, it couldn't have been at a better time," Choyce said as he took his feet off our office desk, then opened a drawer and tossed an envelope on the desktop.

"What's this?" I questioned, then opened it up.

"Okay, Choyce Coleman! I see you wasn't bullshittin', Mr. Real Estate Agent and LLC of His & Hers Realtor's Inc.

"Off top, I told you that you inspired me. Like I said though, thank you, lil' bruh. You saved me, and I owe this new path all to you," Choyce said as he walked over to the window and looked down at our club. We promoted for a week straight to bring the city back out, and it worked. We were filled and still had people lined up down the street to get in.

"Come on, lil' bruh. I want for you to meet the gang. Even though we're out the way, we still got a library and warehouse full of drugs. All them bricks aren't going to sell themselves," Choyce said.

Security came up to grab three case of D'usse,

four case of Gleeko champagne, and a cigar box. Choyce grabbed a bag of jewelry, then we headed out the office.

Choyce took my advice and formulated a team to replace us, since we were no longer in the game. He said they were some hungry go-gettas, that took the streets serious. So, he decided to put them on, and I personally called the one I knew.

We left our office and took the elevator to the first floor. Once the doors opened, we received nothing but love. We walked through the crowd to G Herbo's song *Sessions* until we made it to the lower level VIP. That's where we had the team meet us at.

They already had money, so we didn't have them selling our dope. They just bought our weight instead. We needed them to touch every dollar they could anyway. In the game, you just never knew when you might've needed to bond out of jail, hire an attorney, pay for a funeral, or pay to get a nigga whacked.

Choyce had Lil Black customize iced-out chains with CC emblems. That was for that unity and no man was above the next type shit. Just so they'd feel like they belonged to something that they'd go all out for. He told them to wear all black at the party to represent their power.

"Chance! What's up, bro!" JR said as he rushed over to greet me, and we shook up.

He was my recruit. After what he did with them two-hundred bands and five keys, I had to bring him in.

"Right on for putting me on, and I'm ready to keep the ball rolling for you," JR said.

"Off top, you're up next fo sho, but I want you to meet my bro," I said as I introduced him to Choyce.

"Bro, do you remember when you asked how I got them two niggas, that was on that bullshit with me, to kill each other?"

"Yeah, why, what's good?"

"This is JR, he's the one that helped me pull that shit off."

"Off top, my nigga. That was some real legendary shit. Thanks for helping out my lil' bruh. By doing so, you just helped yourself to the chance of a lifetime. Welcome to the gang," Choyce said as he reached handed him a jewelry box, a fifth, and a bottle of Gleeko.

"Not a problem, that just what real niggas do for one another," JR said as he received his box and opened it.

"Damn! This that drip! Right on, y'all," he said as he placed it around his neck.

"Off top. It's official. Come on and meet the rest of us," Choyce said then walked over.

"Chance, this is the gang. I'm ah start off with Money Man right here. He's out of the Chi and down by law," Choyce introduced.

"This my slime, Streets, he's from Dallas and is ah straight goon wit his. What's good, my nigga?"

"Off top. T-Dot, right here, he's from Candida but grew up in the D. He got that hustle hand like mine."

"And last but not least, my slime, Hell'Rell, a straight killer. He once killed up some opp niggas, came back to the crime scene, and stood next to the eyewitnesses. You see he's still right here, though."

After Choyce passed out the gifts, fifths, and bottles. We all held our D'usse in the sky to pose a toast.

"Hold up, this shit ain't right. Put them fifths down, right quick. I almost forgot," Choyce said as security walked over and passed him a cigar box.

"I had this nigga roll us these blunts of ganja straight from Jamaica. Grab one and a lighter. Light these bitches up, then we'll do a toast.

Everyone grabbed a blunt and lit them up. Once the smoke was in the air, we raised the bottles back up.

"On everything, we gang! None of you niggas are my foot soldiers! We're partners in this shit! It's money to be made out there; we got the supply and demand! All we gotta do is get to it!" Choyce yelled out over the music.

"We're in power, right now! All I suggest is for you niggas to move smooth! And if you get jammed up, don't mention mine or my brother's name! Toast on gang, let's get it!"

Everyone yelled, "Gang!"

We popped the cork on the fifths and Gleeko as we blew on some ganja smoke. The DJ had Jeezy's song *Billions* in a mix as it banged in the background, and the club was lit.

"Come on, lil' bruh. Let's go up to the rooftop and smoke one right quick," Choyce said as he put his arm around my shoulder.

We made it to the top of the building, and it looked like another part of our club.

"Damn bro, you're holding out on me?" I questioned as I looked around.

It had a bar set up, dance floor, DJ booth, and drink tables with bars stools and all. I could see it wasn't finished yet, but it looked nice.

"Nah, Muhammed rented out this space, it's for the twenty-five and over crowd. He got the idea from the Roof Top downtown," Choyce said as he lit up a blunt.

We walked to the corner of the building and looked over. It was lit as fuck down there. The people who couldn't make it into the party, had they own shit going on.

"I'm happy for you, lil' bruh, straight up. When it came to the streets, you handled the game so well, it made me proud. I'm thankful you saw my vision to make us rich and had my back," Choyce said as he passed the blunt to me.

"You know what it is, bro. I saw you weren't the same after Justin got killed. You were at a dark time in your life. I had to be there for because I love you. I know why you chose that path. I was right there, and I couldn't just turn my back on you," I said.

I took a pull from the blunt and blew the smoke in the air. When I looked up, I saw a Lonestar move slowly across the night sky. That was my sign that my job was done, and it was time for me to move on.

"Lil' bruh, the times I thought I lost you were the scariest moments of my life. But you pulled through every time. I prayed that if God got you out of the stuff, I got you into, I'd leave the streets alone."

"I was smart about it and said once what I had left was gone, I'd be done," Choyce said as he laughed.

"But he heard me, that's how I knew he was real. So, get focused, lil' bruh, that football field is calling your name," Choyce said as I passed the blunt back to him.

"Nah, for real. It's long overdue. I got a lot of work to do, but I'm mentally ready for this. Congratulations on your transition though," I congratulated.

"God works in mysterious ways. Who knows, I might've received your karma because God knew it couldn't kill me. The things I did go through that weren't meant for me, gave you a chance to open your eyes and now look at us." Once I finished, I thought back on our journey.

"Off top, and that was a hell of a ride for the both of us. I'm just glad it's over," Choyce said as he put his arm around my shoulder.

"But I told you, by the time you went off to college, I would've taken this city over," He said as he looked over at me with the same smile on his face, he had a couple years ago, when he first made that statement.

If people were to hear our story, they'd say Choyce used me or he ruined my life. What they wouldn't have known was, if I would've turned my back on him, and he would've gotten killed, I would've died on the inside.

When it comes to the ones that you love. You'd never know what you would do for them until you're presented with that situation. What I did for my twin, not only helped us get rich, it helped me to move on with my life, knowing I did all I could do, to be my brother's keeper. But I must admit that was one cold ass summer.

The end!

Thank you for rocking with me! If you would like to enjoy more reads by me Author Courtney B. Check out my catalog.

183

To submit a manuscript to be
considered, email us at
submissions@majorkeypublishing.com